Pearl's a Sinner

K C Carlton

© K C Carlton 2015

K C Carlton has asserted her moral right under the Copyright, Designs and Patents Act 1988 to be identified as the author of this work.

Published by Mandrill Press www.mandrillpress.com

ISBN 978-1-910194-17-1

Also by K C Carlton

Winging It

The Taken By Force Collection Volume 1

Kate Carlton's blog is at http://kccarlton.com/

You can contact her at kc@mandrillpress.com

Chapter 1

"Oh, that I had
Wings of angels
Here to spread and Heavenward fly
I would seek the gates of Sion
Far beyond the starry sky"

The hymn came to an end and that should have been that. With a lightening heart, Pearl rose to her feet and smiled at her mother. Time to go.

But the meeting was not over. Robert Johnson, most senior of the elders if any elder could be said to take precedence over any other, raised his hand. 'I will ask you all, now and in the week ahead, to carry Pearl in your hearts and to pray for her often.' Pearl shivered. What on earth was this? Had she not borne enough for this congregation? 'Pearl will be eighteen on Friday. She is finished with school and sixth form college. At the end of September she will begin her university education. I do not have to tell you how full the world is of temptation and her mother and father, and we her brethren in Christ, will not be there to help. Let us pray that Almighty God will be with her in her time of trial.'

Fury and embarrassment fought in Pearl's breast and both lost to humiliation. In a few days she would be eighteen. An adult. Whatever foolery had gone on among the Brethren, she had gone along with. Being a member of this church, not that you were supposed to call it a church, had cost her any closeness she might have hoped for with other girls. They liked her, or at least she thought they did, but they thought she was potty. 'They are godless people,' her mother said. 'Ignore them.' Which was fine for her mother to say because her mother did not have to go to school. Robert Johnson had stopped speaking and Pearl, her face burning, made for the door.

Dinner on Sundays was in the middle of the day. Roast beef, Yorkshire pudding, roast potatoes, carrots and peas. Gravy.

To drink: water, for no alcohol had ever been served in this house and Pearl had little doubt that it never would be as long as her parents lived in it. Then apple pie with custard (cream would have been far too rich) and a cup of tea.

'Was it not good of Robert Johnson to ask people to pray for you?'

Pearl looked at her mother, careful to allow no hint of distaste to show in her face. 'It was embarrassing.'

'Poor Pearl. You never liked being the centre of attention.'

'Which is a good thing,' said her father.

'You know we worry about you being in a strange city. Here you have people who have known you all your life to support you. There…'

'She has the names of elders where she is going,' said her father. 'She's a good girl. She's been brought up to know right from wrong. You have to trust her.'

Her mother said no more, but her mouth was a thin, straight line.

When Pearl and her brother had left for Bible study, the conversation at home resumed. 'You are so naive,' said Pearl's mother.

'Because I trust my daughter to do what she knows is right?'

'You haven't the faintest idea what it's like to be a young girl. She should be at home, where we can help her until she is safely married.'

'Help her with what?'

'Her *appetites*. Oh, leave it. You will never understand.'

'And you didn't want her to go to university in the first place.'

'That's right. I didn't. I was a young girl once. I know what goes on in that head and you don't.'

'What…'

'I said leave it.'

The day would come when Pearl would look back on her late teen years and be appalled. How could a well brought up young lady possibly have been the seething mass of erotic dreams she remembered? What sort of properly educated damsel spent her time imagining lying naked in the arms of some rampant man? Usually a man she hardly knew or even one she had never met? One day, when she was in a fulfilling relationship with her children about her, she would find the person she had been an unimaginable enigma.

But that day was not now.

She knew that people did not see the real Pearl. She knew that in public she was seen as aloof, even a little on the prim side. She suspected (and of course she was right) that she was by no means the only young woman who presented to the world a picture of calm and propriety that completely hid the sensual reality behind it. Believing that there must be others did not help.

It was wrong. Of course it was wrong. Everything she had been taught since the moment she first understood the simplest words spoken to her told her that God saw what was in her mind. God wanted her to be pure and chaste. She lay in bed and prayed for release from these impure thoughts. She did not want her hand to stray once more beneath the waistband of her pyjamas. She did not want it. She knew what came afterwards: the sadness; the disgust with self; the fear of everlasting hellfire. A terrible death in life.

But God did not hear her prayers. She fought the fight as she always fought it and, as she always did, she lost. She lifted her bottom so that she could get her PJs down, uncovering the place she never should touch.

He wasn't an elder. Elders were usually older than him. She had always called him Uncle. Really, he was a family friend and no blood relation at all but he had been Uncle Martin since her youngest days.

At first he had been the twinkle-eyed man who sat her on his knee, tickled her and made her laugh. By the time she was ten that was at an end; her mother thought it "inappropriate"; but still he made her laugh – by the jokes he told and the way he joined her in surreptitious smiles at her parents' expense. He was ten years younger than they were and less stuffy and she sometimes wondered how they had ever become such good friends. She knew that his wife and her mother had been close as children but now Uncle Martin lived alone and his wife was under discipline which meant that the Brethren were forbidden to break bread with her. They could not have done so if they wished, because no one knew any longer where she was.

And now Pearl was eighteen and Uncle Martin's attitude had changed again. She wasn't a stupid girl; she knew she was attractive, knew that boys at school and then sixth form college would have liked to get into her knickers but she had allowed no liberties. It was easy enough to keep them at arm's length because her religious status was well known. Whatever other girls might do, Pearl did not drink alcohol, dance, smoke or socialise with boys of whom the elders would not approve. Her mother told her how lucky she was and that the rules she lived by kept her free of sin or even the temptation to sin and Pearl agreed with her. Out loud. What went on inside her head was another matter. Her mother feared that, when she got to university, Pearl would be led into temptation and that she would fall. Pearl hoped that she was right.

The glances she sometimes caught on Uncle Martin's face when he thought she wasn't watching suggested that he was as drawn to her as the boys at college and the thought warmed even more than it shocked her – Uncle Martin was thirty-five which was too old altogether, but he was possibly – what was she saying? he was definitely – the best-looking, most desirable man she knew. Maybe Uncle Martin was what she was saving herself for? She shuddered at the thought because she knew it could not be – COULD...NOT...BE – but there was delicious pleasure in the shudder and she would not let it go altogether.

Desirable. Desire. What lovely words. Lovely to her, at any rate. But not to the elders and not to her mother. (Pearl had asked her mother why no elders were women. Was it because none had been deemed worthy? Or were half the population excluded from eldership? Her mother had replied that when

Pearl was older she would see what a silly question that was.)
To the elders, self-respect was a lovely word. Chastity was a
lovely word. And restraint. Boys might achieve these things
for themselves, if they were correctly schooled from their
earliest days, but they were given to girls only in return for
constant prayer. A teacher had said that Muslim men kept
women powerless because they were afraid of them which
was why they covered them from head to foot in black and
denied them any share in governance – of the state; of the
family; of themselves. He had been accused of a hate crime for
saying it and hounded out of his job. Pearl wondered whether
the elders were also afraid of women. Her mother said that,
if so, they were right to be afraid but when Pearl asked for
an explanation she was told only, 'When you're older you'll
look back on the Pearl you are now and you'll understand'.

To avoid hearing conversation about sex at sixth form college
you would have to enter a form of purdah and Pearl was not
prepared to do that. It was bad enough being seen as the
daughter of a family of religious freaks without spending
every second outside the classroom in self-imposed solitary
confinement. There were girls at college who gave themselves
freely and she knew they didn't understand why she held back.
Saving herself. For what, they would ask. It's a membrane.
A piece of skin. Hurts a bit when it's broken but that's soon
forgotten. What do you want? To end up marrying someone
who doesn't know what he's doing, and you don't know
what you're doing, and go through life with a man you've
held yourself back for who isn't as good in bed as some you
might have had?
     There was a teacher at college, a woman, who looked at her
the same way Uncle Martin now did but Pearl gave nothing
back because (1) she didn't want to be branded a lezzie, which
she would be if she even smiled at the woman and (2) she
knew just from looking at the boys in college when they were
changed for rugby or running or even when they were fully
dressed but couldn't – or maybe didn't want to – hide the bulge

in their pants that what she yearned for was something that men and boys had and women didn't. At night in bed after the fruitless struggle with herself she'd act out the fantasies she'd had on and off during the day, imagining a handsome and worldly-wise young man – he was always handsome and worldly-wise, although she didn't actually know anyone, except perhaps Uncle Martin, who fitted that description – talking sweetly to her and telling her how beautiful she was, how desirable, and then kissing her, and unbuttoning her pyjama jacket so that he could stroke her breasts and bring her nipples erect (though really it was her hands and not someone else's that were doing that) before sliding the pants to her knees (she had to lift her bottom so that that could happen) so that his fingers – her fingers, really – could slip into her and play with her and bring her to such a frenzy she was terrified her parents would hear.

And after that the fears of divine retribution and eternal damnation that would keep her awake for hours so that only short hours after she finally did fall asleep her mother would have to bang on the bedroom door to get her to wake, shower, dress and come down to breakfast.

Three weeks after the end of term, the household was woken at four in the morning. Her father answered the phone, her mother went down to join him and the conversation brought Pearl and her brother downstairs too but they were sent back to their rooms. 'Later,' her mother said. 'We'll tell you later.'

Later proved to be breakfast time. Pearl's grandfather had fallen and broken a hip. That would have been a problem in itself; what made it worse was that his wife, Pearl's grand-mother, was in a home suffering from dementia. 'We're going to have to go there,' said Pearl's mother. 'Richard, I'd like you to come with us. You've no school and we are going to need another strong pair of arms to help your father.'

'What about me?' asked Pearl.

'Could you possibly stay here? You can come if you want to but we may be gone a few days and someone needs to water the houseplants and take in the post. Burglars can tell when a house is empty.'

Stay there? Alone? Pearl could think of nothing she'd like more. She nodded. 'Yes. I can do that.'

'Good girl. We'll let the elders know, and Uncle Martin. Nothing will go wrong, but if it does you only have to call him. Richard, as soon as you've finished breakfast Dad will give you a suitcase. Pack enough underwear, shirts, pants and handkerchiefs to last up to a week. And don't forget your washbag. Toothbrush, toothpaste, razor.'

The house was a frenzy of activity for an hour and then it was silent. Pearl walked from room to room, loving a feeling she had never known – the feeling of being alone. Then she returned to the kitchen and set about washing the breakfast things.

At ten o'clock, Uncle Martin drove up to the house.

He'd come to make sure she was all right, she knew that. He was an old family friend and a member of the church and the well-being of every church member was important to every other member. But knowing that didn't stop her from fantasising. Fantasising that he had come to ask for her virginity and fantasising that she would surrender it to him. Eagerly. Without even the pretence of resistance.

When she opened the door, she knew that she was blushing. 'Hello,' she said, and could have kicked herself when she heard how faintly – how shyly – it came out. 'Mummy and Dad have gone to look after grandad.' He was carrying a small bag and she wondered what was in it.

'I know that, sweetheart. I came to see you. Make sure you're okay.'

'Oh.' She stood back to let him in. He walked straight into the kitchen, where he had sat so many times with all four of them, and sat down. 'It's coffee time,' he said. 'Don't you think?'

'I...yes. I was just going to make some.' She hadn't been but now it seemed such an obvious thing to do. She filled the kettle and switched it on. As she stood with her back to him she was conscious of how short her skirt was (though to the girls at college it would have ranked almost as a midi) and how her bottom flared beneath it. She put chocolate biscuits on a plate and set it in front of him.

'Thank you.' He opened the bag and took out a bottle of champagne, still so cold from the fridge that beads clung to the outside like dew. Pearl put her hand to her mouth. 'Oh, my goodness. Is that…?'

'Champagne. I know your grandfather is in hospital and that's a dreadful thing, but you just left college, you're eighteen, you're about to go to university which will change your whole life and I worried that no one was paying enough attention to you. So I thought we'd forget for a while the trouble your parents are attending to and have a little celebration of all the good things in your life. Can you find a couple of glasses?'

Pearl took two tumblers from a cupboard. 'I'm sure these aren't right, but this is all we have. Champagne isn't drunk in this house.'

Champagne wasn't drunk in that house. Martin knew that, all right. The elders didn't ban alcohol as long as you drank it in moderation but they preferred that you went without. Just as they preferred that there be no salt in your food or excitement in your life. Those were preferences. They had other things that were more than preferences; they were rules to be insisted upon, and Martin intended to break one of those rules today. If he could. He wouldn't use force because he wasn't going to be accused of rape but he'd watched this girl grow from a child to where she was now – trembling on the verge of womanhood – and he couldn't help himself. If he could have her without forcing the issue then have her he would. If anyone was to blame it was her for being so beautiful and her parents for keeping her so innocent. It was always the woman who was to blame; political correctness meant that you weren't supposed to say so any more, but everyone knew it was true. A man was helpless in the face of leggy coltishness like Pearl's. That skirt hugged her in a way he was sure her mother had never intended when it was bought. Beneath the skirt would be virginal white cotton knickers and beneath the knickers…

God, he hoped she didn't have her period. Then he chastised himself for using God's name in that way – but he still hoped she didn't have her period.

He prised the cork from the bottle and poured some into each glass. She got more than he did, and not by accident. He raised a glass and touched it to hers. 'Here's to you, Pearl. May your future unfold exactly as you would wish.'

When Pearl drank, a great gulp that half emptied her glass, he took a sip from his own and topped hers up. Her first alcohol. Was he imagining it or was there already a slight glaze to her eyes? She took another biscuit and then another glug of champagne. The less she ate, the faster she would be drunk but he wasn't going to move the biscuits away. That would be too risky. He filled her glass again. 'What are you most looking forward to?'

'At uni?'

'Of course.'

'Oh. Well. You know…finding like-minded people and talking to them about things that really matter.'

'Like…?' Her glass was half empty once more and once more he filled it. Her face was pink, her eyes unfocused and her voice was beginning to slur. This latest top-up should be enough. He didn't want her throwing up – that would ruin everything.

'Well.' She seemed to have difficulty in marshalling her thoughts. 'Literature. Poetry.'

'You're going to be reading history, aren't you?'

'Yes, but…I can still read whatever I want to…what I really want is to be with people like me.'

Better stay in the church then, he thought, and steer clear of educated people. He didn't say it, though. This was not the best time to remind her of religion.

She put the glass down with a clatter. 'Gosh. That was nice. I feel…I feel just a little bit squiffy.'

He walked round the table and took her chin between

thumb and forefinger, raising it so that he could kiss her on the lips. For a moment there was no reaction and then her hands were on his shoulders. They weren't trying to push him away. He'd got the measures about right, then. The colt was about to be broken and it would be done with the colt's wholehearted participation. He pressed with his tongue, her lips opened and tongue twined with tongue. He put both arms around her and raised her to her feet. She pressed against him. Women of the Brethren did not wear perfume but this scent he savoured was of cleanness, soap, shampoo – and something else. Something musky. A scent that had brought man and woman together since they were barely out of the oceans. He kept one arm around her waist, turned her sideways and led her out of the kitchen and towards the stairs. She went willingly, her head resting on his shoulder. The bag he had brought with him was in his other hand.

The room he took her to was her parents' bedroom and not hers. She made no objection because the bed here was larger than her own. As soon as he had closed the door behind them he turned her to him, took her face in his hands and kissed her. He lifted her and placed her on the bed. She lay back, smiling at him. 'You'll be gentle, won't you? This is my first time.'

'I'll do my best, angel.'

Her head was muzzy but it was a nice muzziness. This was like one of her fantasies, the way he undid the blouse buttons one at a time before laying it open, slipping the brassiere up and putting his hands on her breasts. Her own arms lay out to the sides, hands palm upwards as he rolled the taut nipples under his hands and all the time he was kissing her, kissing her, kissing her. Just as she thought she could bear no more dallying he began moving down her body, his lips lingering first at her breasts and then at her navel as his hands found the fastener on her skirt and she lifted her bottom to help him remove it and lifted it again as he drew her knickers down to her ankles and threw them aside. He raised himself on his arms and looked down at her. 'This is make your mind up time,' he said. 'If you want me to stop, say so now. Later, I may not be able to.'

She reached up and drew his head down so that she could kiss him. 'Just don't hurt me.' Was she drunk? She certainly felt woozy but, no, she wasn't drunk. She was allowing it to seem that she might be to excuse what she was doing. Excuse it to him and excuse it to her. She had dreamed of this moment – this time – this act and she knew it was wrong, knew that neither of them should be here in this room and on this bed and if she could feel afterwards that it hadn't been her fault, that she'd had too much to drink, that she would never have let him do what she intended to let him do if she had been sober then she would be able to live with herself. How God would feel about it, she preferred right now not to wonder.

He took a towel from the bag in which he had brought the champagne, folded it and placed it under her bottom. Then he pressed her knees apart and his head was between her thighs and he was kissing her there and now the alcohol was irrelevant because she was on fire and she was shrieking, and shrieking even more as his tongue pressed between the tender folds, and she buried her hands in his curly hair as he licked the whole joyous length of it and then his lips were on the tight little nubbin in which all of her pleasure seemed to be centred while a finger entered her and slid in and out of that molten seat of bliss and she wrapped her thighs tightly round his head as she bucked uncontrollably and screamed and convulsed in unbelievable orgasm.

She fell back, utterly fulfilled. 'Thank you,' she whispered. 'Oh, thank you.'

He smiled and lay beside her, hugging her to him. After a while, and marvelling at her own audacity, she put a hand on him. He was bigger than she had ever imagined and she felt a sudden shiver at the thought of being entered by such a thing in her most precious and tender place, but she put those thoughts from her. 'Are we going all the way?' And where had that expression come from? That was the sort of thing girls and boys had said when she was barely into her teens.

'Do you want to?'

She nodded.

He took one final item from the bag and held it up. 'We don't want any unplanned after-effects, do we?' Pearl knew what this was because sex education at school had been thorough, at least on the mechanics of the act though nothing had been said about feelings, and she had seen a packet just like this opened before the contents were unrolled onto a plastic thing that didn't look much like what she had just held in her hand. 'Really,' he said, 'these bring most pleasure when they can move on...on what's inside them. Which happens when what's inside them has been lubricated. I could use K-Y Jelly, but spit is better.'

It took a moment to understand what he was saying. Was he asking her to spit on him down there? Of course not. She pressed him onto his back, moving with care because her head was spinning just a little, more than a little if she were honest, took his manhood in her hand at the base and slid it into her mouth. This was no mystery, for the girls at college had discussed it often. It felt unbelievably strange, and yet so natural, to have him in her mouth and she set about it with delight until he gently eased her head away and reversed their positions, placing her once more on her back. She watched as he rolled the condom into place and then his tip was at the lips of her sex, and then it was inside her, and however big it had felt and looked it was not too big for the place it found itself in, and then he stopped moving and he was kissing her and his hands were on her breasts and stroking her bottom and she realised that he didn't need to move because *she* was moving, her hips egged on by his hands and her simple lust to be possessed, and he went on kissing her, on the lips and on the throat and on her face and back to her lips, and in he was drawn, and in, until suddenly he hesitated and she knew that he had found the barrier of her maidenhead and she was about to pass from girl to woman and she wrapped her arms around him and squeezed and there, it was done, he was all the way inside her and there was pain as other girls had said there would be but it didn't matter, it would pass, and he had started to move, in and out, faster and faster, and still he kissed her and when she looked into his eyes she saw there a look of tenderest desire and then he was crying out and she knew that he had spent inside the condom and he took his weight on his own arms and he kissed her and kissed her and kissed her and Pearl felt that she had never been so happy, so fulfilled, so female in her life.

They lay side by side, nuzzling each other and murmuring sweet nothings, for what seemed an age and in fact was a long time because when Uncle Martin looked at his watch he said, "One o'clock. I think that's lunch time, don't you?'

Chapter 2

Later she would wonder how a friend of her parents could have taken advantage of their absence like that. Later she would ask herself whether a grown man experienced in the way of the world should have been so carefree with an innocent young maid's virginity. Later. Right now, all she could think was that at long last she had given herself and it had been even more wonderful than people said it would be. And if that didn't prove she'd been right to withhold herself from the boys at college while she waited for the experience and touch of the fabled older man, then what would?

She expected Uncle Martin to take her back to bed that afternoon and was surprised when he did not. He said, 'You're a little sore, Pearl. Aren't you?'

She nodded.

'You'll go on being a little sore for a couple of days and I don't want to make that worse. What I don't want most of all is to make my lovely darling afraid to make love. Because that's what we did, Angel; we didn't have sex – we made love. And I want to make love to you and with you again and again, and it will be nicer if you're always enjoying it and don't have in the back of your mind the time I hurt you by coming into you before the tear was healed.'

It made sense and she knew he was thinking of her, but a girl who has just become sexually active for the first time – and loved every moment of it – doesn't want to give up easily the chance of more and greater pleasure. 'Isn't there anything we can do?'

'You've probably heard your friends talking about sex by the back door?'

Bright red once more, she nodded. 'Once or twice. Some of them.'

'And they didn't really enjoy it, did they? They might have said they did but they didn't fool you?'

'No, I don't think they did. I think they did it for the boy.

I think it hurt.'

'I'm sure it did. That kind of intercourse is something men do to women because they can. They do it to show that they are in charge, that they are the dominant person in the relationship. Well, I don't want to be the dominant person, I want us both to enjoy what we're doing equally although really I know that can never be, and so I won't do that to you. We can use our lips and our tongues; we've already done that and I think you enjoyed it. Well, the way you yelled when I went down on you makes me certain you did, and I don't think you minded taking me in your mouth.'

It was amazing, after what they'd done together, that she could still blush so easily. Quietly she said, 'It was lovely. I didn't think it would be but it was. I felt like a woman giving her man pleasure.'

'And so you did. And we'll do it again, I promise. Tomorrow – are you doing anything tomorrow?'

'I won't be doing anything that doesn't involve you. And that goes for every day until Mummy and Dad get home.'

'I imagine they'll call you this evening?'

'They said they'd call at five every day. Just to tell me what's happening and make sure I'm okay.'

'Then we must be here so they don't suspect anything. But if you like I'll take you to my place afterwards and we can spend the night together.'

She stepped into his tender embrace, pressing her face tight against his chest. 'That would be lovely.'

As they waited for the phone call, Pearl packed a bag with the few things she'd need: her toiletries, her pyjamas (she blushed once more for something so plain seemed unfitting to her new status as mistress – could she call herself a mistress? – she would, whether she should or not) and, for tomorrow morning, a clean pair of knickers and a blouse. She decided that the skirt would do another day. Then she added another pair of knickers because, if they went on getting as damp as they had today, one would not be enough.

In the kitchen, standing beside the phone, she felt Uncle Martin's arms come round her from behind. It felt so safe to stand here being hugged by this strong, masculine man who had fulfilled her dreams. She felt something else, too, and it was pressing into her bottom. She had given up feeling astonished at herself; you accepted what you were or you didn't and Pearl did not see the point in denying herself. She turned to face him, paused just long enough to kiss him on the lips and dropped to her knees. Her hand went to the zipper on the front of his pants. 'I don't think this will wait till tomorrow.' She pulled down the zip and opened with her two thumbs the space at the front of his boxer shorts. She heard his sigh as he burst forth. She did not think she had ever seen anything so beautiful, so male – and it was here, now, for her. She took it into her mouth, drawing it in as far as she could and running her tongue around the hard shaft. How could she ever have told herself that this man was not for her? Maybe this, and not university, was the right thing for her: to stay in her home town, marry Uncle Martin, look after him and raise his children. All her dreams, all her fantasies came together as she took the base of his sex between thumb and forefinger while with the other hand she cupped his balls and allowed her fingertips to stroke the soft skin behind them. The cries he was uttering now were anything but adult, anything but in control. She increased the pressure of the stroking as she sucked harder and harder and suddenly her mouth was flooded with his hot and salty seed.

And at that very moment, the telephone rang.

Holding a finger to his lips, for he was still moaning in ecstatic delight, she picked up the handset only realising at that moment that her mouth was still full of his ejaculation. Her mother's voice was clearly audible. 'Pearl? Are you there? Are you all right?'

She swallowed as fast as she could. 'I'm fine, Mummy. I had to run to get here. I'm a little breathless.' She heard a smothered laugh close beside her. 'How is Granddad?' Uncle Martin's hand rested for a moment on her bottom while the other slipped beneath the hem of her blouse and rose to stroke her nipple into life. She gasped and tried to push his hands away. He kissed her on the back of the neck, leaving both intrusive hands where they were.

'It's going to be a long haul, darling,' said her mother. 'It's a bad break and he's in a lot of pain. A fall like that takes a lot of getting over at his age. We must hope for the best and pray. God knows better than us what Granddad needs. Are you looking after yourself?'

'Of course I am. I'm having a little adventure. I just ate something I've never had before.' Another smothered laugh just behind her ear and then the hand that had rested on her bottom slipped below her skirt. His other hand joined it and she felt her knickers being pulled down.

'Oh? What was it? Something from the supermarket?'

She smothered a scream. 'I'll tell you all about it when you get home. But you don't get things like this in a supermarket.' She lifted one foot and then the other to allow the knickers to be completely removed and then his hands were on the inside of her knees, pressing them apart, and then they were moving gently upwards, sliding over the smooth skin of her thighs until his fingertips came to rest between the quivering lips of her sex. She almost screamed with pleasure as one finger found its way inside her.

'What is it?' asked her mother. 'What's the matter?'

'Nothing. Nothing, Mummy. It was a sneeze, a sneeze I couldn't control. You don't suppose I'm getting hayfever, do you? I've never had it before.'

'Well, it does sometimes come on in early adulthood. But it may be a summer cold or even flu. Take care of yourself, darling. You've made sure you are properly covered up, haven't you?'

'Oh, yes, Mummy. I've been properly covered up all the time.' And now his head was beneath her skirt and his lips kissed her there and his tongue snaked out and ran the length of her vulva, pausing at the top to rattle the tight little button that even now was beginning to grow. Pearl wrapped her thighs around his head in a vain attempt to make him stop long enough for the phone call to be concluded but that tongue would not be stilled. With a sigh of relief she heard her mother bringing the call to an end.

'Dad is calling; I have to go. I'll ring again tomorrow, same time. Look after yourself, darling, and keep warm. These summer colds can be treacherous.'

With relief, she placed the handset back on its rest. Uncle Martin had his hands on her bottom and, as he stretched himself out to lie on his back, he drew her down towards him. One of her knees was on each side of his body. As she came down towards him he slid along the floor so that his face was immediately beneath her. She realised where he was guiding her and she let it happen. As she settled over him, moist and open, his tongue came out and began to lick. She was bobbing up and down in a natural and joyous reaction and he tightened his grip to hold her in place while his tongue brought her to a climax even more intense than the one she had experienced earlier. When he realised that it was over, he moved her until she was lying prone on top of him, face to face. He kissed her.

'How could you do that while you knew I was talking to Mummy? It's a wonder she didn't realise what was going on.'

'So. You've been keeping yourself fully covered up, have you? That isn't how it looked to me.'

'What did you want me to tell her? That her old friend my UNCLE Martin had taken my knickers off? And then taken ME?'

He kissed her again. 'You were a trouper. When you get to uni, join the acting club. I know the elders wouldn't approve but you're a natural. I think we both need a shower. We can have one here, but I have a wet room big enough for us both to get into at the same time.'

'Let's go to your place.'

They were naked under the cascade of hot water in the spacious area that Uncle Martin called his wet room, with tiled walls and a floor that would not let wet feet slip. 'Why did you say we could never enjoy each other equally?'

'When did I say that? Oh, yes, I remember.' He took the soap from her hand and began to rub it over her breasts. 'Well, my dear, it's just one of the differences between men and women. Differences in which women have all the advantages.'

'Oh?'

'I'm afraid so.' He let the jet of hot water wash the foamy lather from her upper body and then turned his attention to her bottom. 'Women can have orgasm after orgasm and men can't.'

'Oh!' The exclamation was prompted partly by what he had told her, and especially the promise of repeated orgasms, and partly by the fact that his finger, covered in soap, had slid into her bottom. 'Oh, Uncle Martin! Oh, that feels so good.'

'Pearl my darling, do you think there might be something a little strange about your calling me uncle while I'm doing this?' Without removing the finger from the silken passage in which he massaged her, he brought the other hand to caress her sex. 'Might you call me just plain Martin?'

She leaned into him, pressing her back against his chest. 'I do see what you mean…Martin.'

'Good.' He withdrew his finger, rubbed the soap once more into the cleft between the cheeks of her bottom, and replaced it. She tilted her head so that, still locked against him, she could offer her lips to be kissed.

'There's more than that. When a man has emptied himself, he needs time to make more seed. The older he gets, the more time he needs. Women's bodies know nothing of that. Do you like it when I do this?'

"This" must mean his use of fingers fore and aft. 'It's wonderful,' she breathed.

'That's good, because when we are dry and horizontal I shall show you something else that I think you'll like even more.'

She knew he would not let her fall and so Pearl simply relaxed as his hands pleasured her. Before long, as he had promised, she felt yet another orgasm rising within her. Her legs parted, seemingly without her willing it, and she cried aloud as the waves of delight passed over her. She sank to her knees to take him into her mouth but he raised her once more to her feet. 'That is what I'm talking about. I'm not ready.'

He turned off the flow of water and led her out of the door to where towels warmed on a rail. He took one and wrapped it around her, patting her dry. Then he dried himself and they walked, naked and hand in hand, through the house and up the stairs into his bedroom. He picked her up and laid her on the bed as he had earlier but this time face down and she wondered whether he had changed his mind about what he had called back door sex. From the drawer from which he had taken a condom he now extracted a small blue tube. 'This is K-Y jelly,' he said. 'You don't lubricate in the back the way you do in front so I have to do it for you. Soap worked before; now this.' He smeared some of the clear jelly on his finger and slid it into Pearl's bottom. It felt as wonderful as it had in the wet room. 'You like that?'

'I love it.'

'Good. Now I want you to turn onto your back without disturbing my finger.'

It took careful manoeuvring to do that but when she was on her back and looking up at him his finger was still in place. He bent his face to the space between her legs and began to work with his tongue as he had done earlier but this time with his finger moving firmly in and out between the cheeks of her bottom. If it had been wonderful before, there was no word to describe how it felt now and she was soon moving, her thighs clasped around his head and her hips bucking so hard she was afraid of throwing him off. Her climax was only moments away and when it came it was volcanic. He lifted himself from her and she lay, almost sobbing with the ecstasy she had just experienced. 'There,' he said. 'I told you you would enjoy it.'

Dinner was a grilled steak and salad, followed by cheese. Martin said, 'I'll never be the cook your mother is but I know how to do simple things. And I think you'll enjoy this wine.' After dinner they had coffee, Martin loaded the dishwasher and they went to bed. He, who slept in nothing at all, said not a word about her PJs.

They fell asleep in each other's arms but it was not as comfortable as it might have been and when Pearl woke shortly after midnight she had her back to him and his arms were round her in a loose embrace. It was a time for reflection and Pearl thought about the experiences of the day and the way they had changed her. She had expected to enjoy being made love to and she had been right. If she chose, she could see herself as a tart, a girl no better than she should be as her mother might have said. She did not so choose. She was doing what other girls did, she had little doubt that the man she was doing it with was a better lover than any they had, and she was happy – happy to be no longer a virgin, happy to be fulfilled, happy to have been shown the way by an experienced man instead of by a boy who knew no more than she did.

And yet. Even in her satisfied state, she could still fantasise about other ways of being. She had been the pupil and Martin the teacher. At this stage of her life, that was as it should be, but she was aware that there were other dreams; dreams in which she took charge and showed an innocent young man how to please her. As she drifted once more into sleep, she had a mental image that was almost shocking. An image in which she undressed a boy and took him as Martin had taken her. The reason that picture seemed shocking was that the pants she rolled down the boy's thighs were a girl's knickers and not Y-Fronts or boxer shorts. Did that mean that she was a lezzie after all? No, it did not. There had been girls in college whose leanings were towards other girls and not men or boys and she had had no problem with that. But she knew, as she had known when the teacher looked at her in that way, that she would not be content unless the person in bed with her was male, with the assets of a male. Perhaps, though, beneath his outer layers he might not always dress as one.

But if she married Uncle Martin, that was one dream that would never come true. Was this how the adult world was? A series of choices that you had to make, where each, however desirable in itself, closed the door on some other that was equally rewarding?

When they woke, it was once more as though Martin knew the fantasies she had had and was playing them out for her because he unbuttoned her pyjama jacket in exactly the way she had imagined and fondled her breasts just as she had hoped before beginning the removal of her pants.

'Martin, darling, stop! I need to pee.'

He hopped out of bed, took her hand and led her onto the landing. She blushed as brightly as she had in all the time they had been together. 'You're not going to watch!'

'Why not? After everything we've done together, are you too embarrassed to let me see you wee?'

The question was a sensible one but her blushes did not fade as he knelt before her watching the stream that tinkled into the bowl. Beside it was a bidet and without argument she let him sit her on it, wet a facecloth and wipe her sex clean. She was just as passive as he dried her. She thought about her situation. Yes, she had been embarrassed but now she knew that she was once more clean and sweet and that must surely make his pleasure greater. Of her own coming satisfaction she had not the slightest doubt. Nor was doubt needed, for his tongue brought her to ecstatic climax as easily as before.

When it was over, she held his face between both hands and looked him in the eye. Something had been troubling her and she had to know. 'Don't I taste horrible down there?'

Martin laughed. 'Darling. If I didn't like it, I wouldn't do it.'

She supposed that must be true.

It would be easy to write more of the same and a series of sex scenes would certainly be a realistic representation of Pearl's life during the rest of the time her parents were away, but the most exciting thing repeated again and again becomes boring; there would be little additional pleasure in it for the reader and none at all for the writer. Let us, then, simply say: that Pearl was the willing recipient of Martin's fingers, tongue and penis during that time. She also came to know rather more about wine than she had a few days earlier.

The first hint of disaster came the day after her parents and her brother came home. They had arranged at some cost for a private ambulance to transfer her grandfather the hundred and fifty miles from his home town and bought a bed of the kind used in hospitals which they had set up in the sitting room. 'I know it isn't ideal,' said her mother, 'but what else can we do? I'd ask you and Richard to share a room, not that that would be at all suitable, but how would Grandad get up and down the stairs?'

Pearl supposed that they would survive; she'd always liked her grandfather and there were not many weeks to go before she set off for university. If, that is, she went for she still harboured dreams of marriage to Uncle Martin.

He came to visit, ostensibly to welcome the travellers home and say hello to the old man but he wore a look of anxiety and did not stay long – just long enough, in fact, to whisper to Pearl, 'Call me. Not from here. Go to a phone box.'

'I could come to your place? It isn't far.'

'*No*! Whatever you do, stay away from there.' And with a quick round of goodbyes he was gone.

'Darling,' she said as soon as she had been able to excuse herself and find somewhere from which to phone. 'What is it?'

'Rhona Hargreaves saw us.' Rhona Hargreaves was the wife of an elder and one of the nosiest of the church women.

'What do you mean, saw us?'

'She saw me coming out of your place. Twice. She saw you coming out of my place.'

Pearl's heart felt filled with lead. Rhona Hargreaves would not see a man and a young woman in love, and nor would the elders. What they saw would be sexual immorality. In their eyes there could be no greater offence. Even murder was not a bigger crime.

'They hauled me in front of the elders this morning.'

'Well, what did you say? No one can prove anything. And how did the woman see so much? What was she *doing* there?'

'Oh, what do you think she was doing there? She saw us once and she set out to spy.'

'Well, how did it go? You denied doing anything wrong?' There was silence at the other end of the line. 'Martin? What…'

'They're going to put you into discipline. I shouldn't have come near your place but I had to warn you.'

Pearl put a hand against the glass at the side of the kiosk to hold herself upright. 'Me? They're putting me into discipline? What about you? Did you tell them it took most of a bottle of champagne to get me into bed?'

Martin's voice was cold. 'There was no champagne, Pearl. And if you say there was, I'll deny it. Go home now. Your parents will be hearing from the elders.'

She walked home hardly knowing what she was doing. She was at the phone box and then she was at her front gate but how she got from one to the other or how long it took she could not have said. When she let herself in, she knew that the worst had already happened. Richard was there and her grandfather was there but her parents were not.

'What have you been doing,' Richard said. 'While we were away?'

She slumped into a chair. 'Why?'

'Mummy and Dad have been called to a meeting. It's about you. That's all they were told. Pearl, you look awful. What's happened?'

She shook her head, unable to speak.

'Would you like me to make you a cup of tea?'

Pearl nodded. 'That would be wonderful. Thank you.' But when the tea arrived, she was unable to drink it.

Chapter 3

It was hard to believe. When the elders said that no one was to break bread with Pearl until she had repented and been forgiven, "no one" included her own family. 'Where am I supposed to eat?'

'In the kitchen,' her mother said. 'So long as we're not in it. If we are, you'll eat in your room.'

They circled each other, her mother's eyes as full of pain as was Pearl's heart. If her father attempted to intervene, her mother chased him away.

'Seducing an older man,' her mother said. 'Oh, Pearl. How could you?'

'He was the one who seduced me. He brought a bottle of champagne to do it with.'

'You drank alcohol, too. Don't you see, that only makes it worse?'

'So what about him, Mummy? Is he in discipline, too?'

'Oh, Pearl. Girls becoming young women have such power over men and often they don't know they have it. That's why I tried to bring you up the way I did; to understand your power and not to abuse it. Uncle Martin admitted responsibility to the elders. He repented. Which you must also do.'

Pearl swallowed. She knew the gravity of what she was about to say. 'I won't. I can't. I'm not sorry for what we did. I thought he loved me. I thought we'd marry.'

'I'm sorry, Pearl, I can't deal with this. Go to your room please.'

'No.'

'I beg your pardon?'

'I won't go to my room. I won't be treated as a child. If I can't stay here and talk I'm going out.'

'Where? Where are you going?'

'I don't know yet. I'll be back for dinner. You can serve it to me where you like. If we had a dog I could eat in the kennel.'

What she was thinking when she left was that she would go

to the places people from college hung out in – she knew their favourite pub, though she had never been in it, she knew the coffee shop they liked and the place in the park where they congregated when the weather was fine. In the end, though, she avoided those places. She didn't want to have to explain away her reddened eyes. She didn't want anyone to know how foolish she had been.

Yet how had she been foolish? She had wanted to give her virginity to someone who would cherish the gift and she had thought that Uncle Martin was that person. If her mind had been fuddled by alcohol that was his fault and not hers.

What she did in the end was to get on the bus that travelled on a circular route all around the city and when it returned after two hours to the place where she had boarded it she got off and walked home. It was clear as soon as she opened the door that her father and mother had been talking and that her father had made a stand. That was something he did rarely but when he made his position clear he brooked no argument. 'Hello, petal,' he said. 'Have you had a nice time?'

She was so grateful to be treated like this that she didn't ask herself why gratitude should be necessary. 'It was okay.'

'Dinner's nearly ready. Come and sit down.'

Pearl looked at the table. Five places were set. At one of them was Granddad's shiny new wheelchair. That left four. 'What will the elders say?'

'I'm not concerned with the views of elders. I'm concerned with the well-being of the daughter I love.'

Pearl threw her arms round his neck, tears rolling down her cheeks. They had never been a hugely demonstrative family because too much emotion was frowned upon but the knowledge that her father would put her before the church overwhelmed her. If an elder called to check – and that was quite likely to happen – the Brethren would be told not to break bread with any of them. They would be put into discipline and ostracised. Sobbing against his neck she said, 'You'll get into trouble. I don't mind eating on my own. Honestly I don't.'

'Well, I mind it. Sit down and let's talk while your mother

puts the finishing touches to the meal.'

Pearl knew what that meant. Her mother had been told to stay in the kitchen until her father had said what he wanted to say and heard what he wanted to know. She knew how much her father loved her mother but she also knew that there were times when he had to overrule her.

'If Martin wanted to marry you, what would you say?'

'I'm eighteen, Dad.'

'Too young, I know. But you thought about it. I suppose that might have been the alcohol.'

'You believe me about the champagne, then.'

'Of course I believe you. He acted the cad and I'm not at all sure that I want him as a son-in-law but very few fathers get the son-in-law they think their daughter deserves. So. If he did want to, what would you say?'

'No. I'd say no.'

'Okay. As long as you're sure.'

'He sold me out to the elders to save his own skin. I wouldn't marry him now if he were the last man on earth. I'm going to uni. I'll get the best degree I can and make you proud of me.'

'You don't need a degree to make me proud of you, girl. Now go and tell the others to get the dinner in here.'

In fact, Pearl did not need to go anywhere to tell her mother to serve dinner because she had been listening at the door and as soon as she heard her husband's words she began carrying dishes to the table. 'I'll eat in the kitchen.'

'Elizabeth…'

'Our daughter is under discipline. We have been told not to eat with her.'

'If the elders told you not to let her in the house, would you obey them?'

'Of course I would. She has sinned, Michael. And she is far from repentance. God makes His rules for our benefit.'

Pearl picked up a knife and fork and carried them into the kitchen.

Chapter 4

The university Pearl had chosen and that had chosen her was in a city nearly two hundred miles from where she had lived her life till now. The time until she would leave home seemed endless but the moment came at last. 'Is anyone going to drive me there? Or shall I go by train?' Her father said, 'I'll take you.'

'Wouldn't it be better if I did?' said her mother.

'Would it? We're going to take a picnic and Pearl and I will eat it together. Would you do that?' Her mother remained silent.

Pearl put her bag, clothes, tennis racquet, books and electronic equipment into her father's car. Twenty miles from their destination they stopped to eat their picnic. Pearl said, 'I'm sorry I've brought such grief on you.'

'Who knows why these things happen? Well, God knows but He rarely shares the information with us.'

'I don't suppose there's any point in my approaching the elders here? The ones whose names I was given before they realised what a slut I was?'

'Please don't use words like that, Pearl. But no. I don't suppose there's any point at all.' He handed her an envelope. 'There's some cash in there, and a cheque. Open an account as soon as you can. You'll need clothes and I suspect your mother might not approve of the ones you buy. Live your life, Pearl. But please don't forget the values you were brought up with. Don't give yourself lightly. You've got my mobile number?'

She nodded.

'If you need money or help or just to talk, call me.'

The tears that had hovered in the background now poured down her cheeks. 'Oh, Daddy. I've come between you and Mummy, haven't I? I've destroyed our family.'

He smiled. 'I think you'll find we're tougher than that.'

At the end of the journey, Pearl helped her father unload the car. He waited long enough to be sure that Pearl had met people and was not totally alone and then left his daughter to begin this new phase of her life.

Pearl's reaction to her new life split into three parts. She loved the academic challenge, but hated what passed for social life. Perhaps, if Martin had not introduced her to the pleasures of the flesh and the enjoyment of good wine, things might have been different – but he had. She watched the drunken cavorting of her university cohort first with amused disdain and then with active dislike. If she were going to get through these three years without being thought a total prig, the most important task was to find like-minded people. And, underlying all this, was pain at the way she had been dealt with by the religious community on whom she had been brought up to depend.

Her father had told her not to use the word "slut" but that was how she had been treated. Had her fantasies – her desire to give in to the hormones that raged within her – really been so disgraceful? She still had them. She still felt the need to be undressed, petted, stroked and possessed and she struggled to see those desires as sinful. She had spent some of her father's money on shorter skirts, knickers that men might find attractive (though no man had as yet been allowed to see them) and nightwear shorter and sexier than she had been brought up with. At night now she was less prone to resist the temptation to move aside her nightie and put her hand where the teaching of the elders said no hand but that of a lawful husband should ever be permitted. And she still imagined that the fingers bringing her to joyful climax were those of a man and not her own. Something so natural could not be wrong. It had to be her straight-laced religious upbringing and not her own inclinations that were awry. For eighteen years, God and what He wanted had been drummed into her. Had it all been for nothing? If she even thought about this aspect of her life, it was in a spirit of rejection – of the elders; of a society that called itself God-fearing but that thought nothing of ripping up a loving family by ordering them not to eat together; of a faith that taught universal love but only seem to come alive when it found reason to hate. She did not believe she would ever be reconciled with those people.

Something else she had done was to register with a doctor

and get herself put on the contraceptive pill. She took it every day. She had not given herself to anyone here and had not even been tempted but she knew that, if the opportunity arose, she could do so without fear. And even that was obfuscation because the opportunity arose almost daily – what was lacking was desire for the man in question.

Of those three parts to her life, the academic ambition proved no difficulty because she studied hard and her essays and contributions at tutorial received praise. Solving the second problem – the need for like-minded people – proved easier than she feared, for she did not have to search her new friends out – they came looking for her. And, as it happened, that also met her third desire by allowing her to meet her sexual needs while at the same time spitting in the elders' faces by doing something they would find outrageous.

It was one of those warm and sunny days when the English summer refuses to accept that autumn is here. Pearl had taken her book, a notepad and a bottle of water onto the grassy banks that sloped from the living accommodation down to the lake with its waterlilies and its ducks and had settled down to prepare an essay.

She had begun to make her first notes when two young women took their place one on each side of her. They were not people that Pearl had ever seen before but she guessed they were two or three years older than her and assumed they must be final year or even graduate students.

'You don't mind if we join you?' said one and only politeness prevented Pearl from saying that it didn't seem to matter whether she minded or not and that, actually, she had work she needed to do when the other woman said, 'Only we've been watching you.'

'Oh?'

'You don't seem to spend much time with your peers.'

What Pearl thought was that she didn't regard most of the boys and girls – they weren't grown-up enough for her to think of them as young men and women – as her peers but, once again, politeness ruled her tongue.

'We wondered whether perhaps you found them immature,' said the first woman.

'Oh?' she repeated.

'Are you a virgin?'

'*What*?'

'Forgive my friend's forthright manner,' said the second woman. 'I'm Evelyn, by the way. And this is Sandra. We're not interested in your virginity for ourselves; this isn't a Sapphic approach. But we may have something that could interest you...'

'... a different way of spending your leisure time that doesn't involve being with a bunch of people who think getting drunk as fast as possible is the height of sophistication...' said Sandra.

'... and we chose you to speak to because you have an air about you...'

'... one that says you've already experienced greater pleasures than that...'

'... but we have to be a little cautious.'

'If it turns out that you stand apart because you're a religious person...'

'... like if you're planning to be a nun when you graduate...'

'... then we'll have made fools of ourselves, which we don't particularly mind, but we'll have exposed other people to a risk they won't appreciate.'

'And that's something we do mind. So: are you?'

Pearl would wonder, later, what had made her answer so frankly instead of getting up and walking away, but at this moment she was aware of an undirected excitement. Something was being talked about here, something secret and undisclosed but something about which she wanted to know more. 'No,' she said. 'I don't know what on earth you're talking about but no and no. No, I'm not a virgin and no, I'm not thinking of taking the veil. Far from it.'

'Well,' said Sandra, 'that's a start.'

'We won't take more of your time right now,' said Evelyn, 'but we would like to talk later. Are you doing anything this evening?'

'I haven't planned anything.'

'We'd like to give you dinner. Have you tried the dining room at Marianne's?'

'Of course I haven't. That's the best hotel in town and way beyond a student's budget.'

'Budgets don't figure for people who do what we're talking about,' said Sandra. 'We'll reserve a table for three. Eight o'clock?'

It was decision time, and Pearl didn't hesitate. 'I'll be there.'

'Then we'll see you later. Ask for Mayhew.'

They stood, smiled at Pearl and walked away. Still thinking about what they had said about budgets not mattering, she was struck by the quality of the clothes they wore. Casual and nothing that would stand out in a crowd but there was money there. Either they came from wealthy families or…Pearl found that she didn't want to consider that "or" too closely. This evening she would find out what was on offer. And, whether she accepted or not, she could be certain of one thing: that she would have the best meal she had eaten since she got here.

Pearl arrived at Marianne's a few minutes after eight because she did not want to be the first there, although she could not have said why. Was there a flicker of understanding from the front of house lady when she mentioned Mayhew? Perhaps; or perhaps it was simply that her awareness was heightened by the slight nervousness she brought with her. At any rate, she was escorted to a corner table at which Evelyn and Sandra were already sitting. They smiled as she approached and Evelyn patted the chair between them. Front-of-house hovered and Sandra said, 'Pearl. What would you like to drink?'

Pearl's time with Martin had been short, but not too short to give her some basic understanding of wine. 'What are you drinking?'

'A sauvignon blanc,' said Evelyn.

Pearl shivered. 'Too much like gooseberries for me.' She turned to the woman. 'Do you have a chardonnay that hasn't been heavily oaked? Ideally French?'

'Of course, Madame.'

Evelyn was smiling and Pearl knew why, just as she knew why she had refused the sauvignon and expressed a preference of her own. She had wanted to show that she was no innocent beginner and it was clear that Evelyn had received the message.

'Did you get your work done?' asked Sandra.

'It wasn't easy to get back to nineteenth century history after what I'd heard from you two. Or, rather, what I hadn't heard.'

'You'll understand eventually why we weren't able to be open. Aren't able, in fact, because we won't put all our cards on the table until we know you better and have a feeling for how you will react.' A waiter put a glass of wine in front of Pearl and a menu beside her place. 'But let's choose what we're going to eat before we get onto the interview.'

'Interview? Is that what this is?'

'Yes, Pearl. We have a position to offer. One that won't interfere in any way with your studies or your ability to take the good degree that I've no doubt you aspire to. But before we can tell you what it is we have to know beyond doubt that you are qualified.' She picked up the menu and began to read it as though to stress that that part of the conversation was over for the time being. Well, the information would come when it came.

It didn't take long. Pearl was only halfway through her first course (breast of quail with confit leg in a filo parcel, spiced shallot chutney and onion consommé) when she realised how closely Sandra and Evelyn were studying her table manners and she experienced a Eureka moment. They wanted to know that she could conduct herself in polite company. 'Escort,' she said. 'You want me to be an escort.'

Evelyn laughed. 'I told Sandra that you were just about the brightest we'd ever approached.'

'Is that what you two do?' asked Pearl. 'You're escorts?'

Evelyn nodded. 'How do you feel about that?'

Pearl put down her knife and fork. 'Frankly? I find it difficult to see the difference between that and prostitution.'

Sandra said, 'An escort goes on a date with a man. A whore goes to bed with him.'

'Yes? And how often, when you've been on a date a man has hired you for, do you fail to sleep with him?'

Sandra blushed. 'Not often,' said Evelyn.

'In fact, never?'

'Well,' said Evelyn, 'if we made a mistake we made it. Let's enjoy the meal anyway and then we can go our separate ways.'

Pearl knew how calm she must seem to the other two. The reality was very different. Her mind was a mass of contradictory impulses. She knew what was being offered. You could dress it up any way you liked, but she was being asked to put herself into a position where she was likely to find herself having sex with men for money and – shorn of all euphemisms – there was only one word for a woman who did that. On the other hand…and how she wondered how a girl brought up by the Brethren could even think that there was an other hand… she would be the sexually satisfied person she had dreamed of being, she would make enough money to enjoy complete independence – and she would feel that she had won some kind of victory over the spiteful elders who had ruled that no God-fearing person should even sit at the same table with her at mealtimes. She gulped. She summoned all the courage she could find. And then fury over the way the Brethren had treated her filled her as it had done so many times since Uncle Martin had put her dreams into effect and courage became unnecessary. 'Who said you made a mistake?'

Evelyn stared at her for a moment and then began to laugh. 'You like the idea?'

'I have only three conditions.'

'They are?'

'One: that I'll be kept safe. Two: that I'll go to bed only with people who know what they're doing. And three: that the money is satisfactory.' She returned to her plate. 'This is delicious.'

For the next twenty minutes, Sandra and Evelyn discussed

Pearl's conditions. Evelyn said, 'There are lots of people who call themselves escorts. Google the word and you'll see. Google it along with your town and you may be surprised to find some of your neighbours. They'll have a website where they take bookings. That's not how we operate.'

'We work for a husband and wife business,' said Sandra. 'You'd recognise their names but if you don't mind we won't tell you just yet who they are. They're extremely well connected with some wealthy and powerful people and they make our appointments for us. You won't ever be with someone they can't vouch for and nor will you ever be with a client without their knowing. And the client will know that they know and that, if you go missing, the police will be knocking at their door.'

'That means they take part of the fee,' said Evelyn. 'It's worth it for the protection. The client pays them two hundred pounds and you get half of that. A hundred pounds just for going to dinner or a club with a man. Any service you provide,' and she smiled as she used the word "service", 'the client pays you and you keep all of it.'

Sandra took a card from her bag and laid it on the table. 'Sometimes – quite often, really – the client knows what he wants and what the price is. Four times out of five, he'll want you to stay all night, take him in your mouth when he wants you to, take him inside you…'

'… that's Sandra's rather prissy way of saying let him fuck you…'

'… as often as he wants…'

'… and for that you get five hundred pounds.'

Pearl paused with the wine glass half way to her mouth. 'That's a huge amount of money.'

'It is when you compare it with the fifty the girl with the website gets. A hundred at the most. But to the men you'll be fixed up with, it's nothing. They're the only kind we deal with. What they want in return is a classy date they'll be happy to be seen with and the certainty that you're clean and discreet. The one thing a girl on this team must not do is kiss and tell. Do that and we can't protect you.'

'And now Evelyn is the one being prissy,' said Sandra, 'because she talks about the men you'll be fixed up with as though it were only ever men. If you're prepared to go with a woman, you'll be matched with one from time to time. Are you?'

The excitement Pearl had been feeling throughout this conversation intensified. 'I don't know. I've never done that. It's never appealed. But for money…'

'… and the thrill of something new…' said Sandra.

'… I wouldn't rule it out.'

'In any case,' said Sandra, 'that, as I say, is how it goes most often. But sometimes they don't know how to ask for what they want…'

'… or they haven't decided yet,' said Evelyn. 'Just like we hadn't decided what we wanted to eat tonight until we looked at the menu.'

'In which case,' said Sandra, 'this card comes in handy. It tells them what's on offer and what they'll pay if that's what they choose.'

Pearl picked up the card and studied it. 'I don't know what some of these things mean. What's a muff dive?'

'Oh, that just means he goes down on you. You've done that?'

'Oh, yes, I've done *that*.'

'We'll go through everything on the list before you meet your first client. You have decided? You do want there to be a first client?'

Pearl sat back and thought about it. It was, once again, decision time. She had not felt so excited since the first time the man she had still thought of then as Uncle Martin had negotiated the surrender of her virginity. She wondered now how he would have reacted if she had suggested he pay her five hundred pounds. 'Yes. I have decided. Count me in.'

Sandra took back the card and pointed to one line with her finger. 'You'll see that I've drawn a line through that one. It's something I don't do. Won't do. But I leave it on the card and struck out so that, if the client thinks he'd like to do it to me, he knows I'm going to refuse. You don't have to do anything you don't want to do.'

Pearl nodded. 'You mentioned that one of the things the man gets is that he knows I'm clean.'

'You'll be checked once a month. The Doctor is a woman and very discreet. And the men who ask for an escort don't get one until they have provided a medical certificate, too. And while we're on *that* subject, I take it you are on the pill?'

'I am.'

Evelyn raised a hand in the direction of their waiter and a few moments later their main courses arrived. Pearl realised that they had been held back until the bulk of the business discussion was over.

She walked back that night with a stomach alive with butter-flies and a head in turmoil. She had agreed to go on dates with men and to be paid for it. On the face of it, that was all she had agreed to do – but she wasn't in the mood to kid herself; she would also go to bed with them. Was she going to do this simply to satisfy a sexual need that she was unable to deny? Was it the promise of more money than she had dreamed of? Or was she motivated by the anger that got worse and not better as time went on about the way Martin had betrayed her and how the Brethren had responded?

As she turned through the gate, a young man in her own year caught up with her. 'Good evening, Pearl. Been somewhere interesting?'

'I had dinner at Marianne's. Two old friends.'

'Marianne's! Out of my class. What's it like?'

'Out of mine, too. My friends were paying. It's very good, though. Worth the money if you happen to be able to afford it.'

'I've been in the Railway Arms. It's jazz night on Thursdays. You wouldn't like to come with me some time, I suppose?'

No, Trevor, thought Pearl. I wouldn't. It would take more than a pint of beer and a packet of crisps and the promise of some third rate jazz to get me to go anywhere with you. But aloud she said, 'Jazz isn't really my thing.'

'Oh, well. No harm in asking, is there?'

'No, Trevor. There's never any harm in asking.'

Chapter 5

There were times over the next two days when Pearl had to remind herself that she was still a student and that being a student took precedence over being an escort. Evelyn had been right; she wanted to leave with a degree and she wanted it to be a good one. That didn't prevent the anticipation she felt and when she examined it she knew that money was only a small part of that; what she wanted most was the excitement of sex. When Uncle Martin had come to the house, he was acting on something that he had seen in her when it was still half hidden in her own mind – that she was a sexual being, that sex was important to her and that she wanted to lie naked in the arms of a man and have that man possess her. That man. That woman, too? She wasn't sure about that but she was prepared to find out.

At dinner in Marianne's, she had asked about clothes and been told that what she had would be fine for the first dates. 'You won't start with parties or anything else that means you have to be away from here in large groups of people. Your first dates will take place where you can be comfortable. Dinner here at Marianne's, probably, and then the man, whoever he is, will have a room either here or in that lovely country house hotel just outside the town and you'll go there with him. He'll know you're a student. That will be half the fun for him – the idea that he is enjoying a girl in the first flush of womanhood. He won't expect you to have glamorous clothes.'

'If I go to bed with him here, the staff here will know what I am. That lady maître d' – what you call someone like that? A maîtresse d'? – she'll know I'm on the game.'

'I'd rather you didn't use that expression,' said Evelyn, 'but yes. She will know. She knows when one of us does it. She's part of your security. This team you're joining is a far wider network than you may realise.'

'How will I know when I'm going to be wanted?'

'You should expect to be working at least two weekends each month, sometimes more, and after the first two or three dates that will probably mean all weekend. The man will pick you up at an agreed place – we don't want the university authorities watching you go off every Friday evening with a different man – and he'll bring you back sometime on Sunday. Other than that, you'll have the occasional weekday night.' She took out her phone, pressed some buttons and Pearl heard her own phone beep in her handbag. When she looked at it there was a message. *Saturday. 8 PM. Marianne's. Desmond Payne.* 'That's how we'll let you know you have a date. And that wasn't just a workout – Desmond Payne will be expecting you this Saturday at Marianne's at eight.'

'Desmond Payne! But he's…'

'We know who he is, Pearl. But if anyone sees you with him, he's an old friend of your family who happened to be in the area and invited you to dinner. Yes?'

'Well…yes. Good grief. Desmond Payne.'

And it was with thoughts of Desmond Payne – the famous, gorgeous, powerful and rich Desmond Payne – that Pearl's mind had been filled when she told Trevor that she was not interested in joining him at the Railway Arms. Those same thoughts had occupied her mind on and off ever since Evelyn had named the man. 'Why does a man like Desmond Payne need an escort?' she had asked. 'He must have his pick of women.'

'He does. And the women make sure that the paparazzi have been tipped off because they all want careers as models or actresses and they think appearing in *The Sun* on the arm of a man like that will help them. In other words, they are using him. He knows that, it's part of the game and generally he accepts it but sometimes he wants what only someone like me or Sandra or you can offer him – a straightforward coupling with no conditions and no aftermath and no journalists sticking lenses in his face.'

'But the press will know he's here?'

'How? He'll arrive in a blacked out limo. Eloise isn't going to tell anyone. That's her name by the way – the woman you called the maîtresse d'. It isn't only the food and the Egyptian cotton sheets that make Marianne's so famous. There's more real privacy here than almost anywhere on earth. But he will want you to leave before breakfast so that he comes down alone. A driver will take you back to college. Have your breakfast there, do it publicly by which I mean eat breakfast even if you don't happen to want it so that people see you doing it and they'll know you got home that night, and if anyone asks just tell them the story: old family friend, invitation accepted for your father's sake, lovely evening, nice man, wouldn't dream of taking liberties. Okay?'

And now Saturday was here, it was five o'clock and in three hours she was to present herself at Marianne's where Eloise would escort her to the table of old family friend Desmond Payne who in due course would take her naked into his bed and have sex with her. She laughed aloud when for the first time she saw the connection – Uncle Martin had been an old family friend and he, too, had taken her naked to bed and had sex with her. A neat conjunction.

She showered. Really, she would have preferred a long luxurious soak in the bath but there were only showers in the accommodation block. Back in her room, she put on clean knickers and a bra and shaved her legs. While she was doing this, there was a knock on the door and Helen's voice shouted through it to ask whether she wanted to go for dinner at a house rented by three second year students. Pearl liked Helen and it was an invitation she would certainly have accepted had she not been otherwise booked. She called out, 'I'd love to, but an old friend of my father has invited me to dinner and I couldn't get out of it.'

'Oh, no! Poor you. Where is he taking you?'

'Marianne's.'

'Oh! Not so poor you. Well, enjoy it. I expect your food will be better than I get even if the conversation is a bore.'

Very carefully, Pearl painted her finger and toe nails and waited for them to dry before picking out her best blouse and her best pair of jeans. If Desmond Payne wanted the virginal young student look, that's what he would get. But what if he wanted to undress her? Which he would. Wouldn't he? Would jeans make that easy? She took them off again and picked out a loose knee-length cotton skirt.

She became aware that she was dreaming and what she was dreaming of was suspenders: specifically, a suspender belt and stockings. That would round out the picture of the sexual being – the sexual being that she had become and the one that she wanted Desmond Payne to see. How had she got here? Had Uncle Martin seduced her? Well, yes, of course he had in the sense that he had persuaded her to go to bed with him, but that had not happened in a vacuum. He had only been able to get her knickers off because she wanted them off, as long as the man was right. And Uncle Martin had seemed to be the right sort of man, even if his later actions had proved otherwise. This was who she was and who she had been for longer than she had been aware of it.

It was only then that she began to think seriously about what it was that she planned to do. She sat on her narrow bed, hands clasped in her lap, and let the feeling wash over her. She was about to give herself to a man she had never met. For money. That made her a…she didn't want to use the word. But it did. Didn't it? Only a…only one of those women she didn't want to name would do what she planned to do. Wouldn't they?

And what would the elders say? And would they be right? She shook her head. The elders had done their best to wreck her family, they had treated her – a young woman led astray by an experienced older man with a bottle of champagne – as a harlot. (And, if that was not quite the way it had been, that was how she had made up her mind to see it). The elders could go to the devil.

In any case, she had no suspender belt and no stockings. Next time, she told herself; next time, she would have. There was an Ann Summers shop in town and, if they couldn't provide what she sought, she would find something online. For tonight, though, it would have to be bare legs because, even if it had not been such a warm evening, she doubted that any man would find tights to be anything other than sexless.

It was two minutes to eight when Pearl walked through the front door of Marianne's and approached the dining room. She had wanted to be late for the meeting with Evelyn and Sandra; for Desmond Payne she meant to be exactly on time. She knew why. The meeting with the two young women had been social. This was business. She was here as…a professional lady. (She still did not feel able to use the word the world would use).

Eloise met her with a smile such as one might give an old friend and escorted her to the table where Payne was already sitting. He rose from his chair as she approached and held out his hand. The smile on his face told anyone who might be watching that he was greeting someone who mattered to him – not someone he planned to pay to spend the night in his bed. Of course, he was an actor. Nevertheless, the smile was genuine. Wasn't it? She could allow herself to think so, at any rate.

He took her hand in his, kissed her on the cheek (the scent of lime and cinnamon on his own cheek was faint, as it should be, but it was there) and fussed her into her seat. 'A drink? I'm having a glass of champagne, but please…ask for whatever you would like.'

She smiled inwardly at the thought of what champagne had already done to her. 'Champagne would be lovely, thank you.'

She was aware of eyes on them all around the room. This must be what it was like to be famous. They had private dining rooms at Marianne's, she knew that, but using one of those would belie the picture her host wanted to show the world of a meeting between old family friends. Everyone knew what went on in private dining rooms. Everyone had known since the days of the Hell Fire Club three centuries earlier.

And then she realised that she was having these thoughts because she was nervous and she asked herself what there was to be nervous about. One thing was obvious and that was that this man she had only just met was very soon going to part her thighs and take her. Yes, that was just cause for nervousness. But as for the rest – the things that were really in her mind right now – the women watching her with obvious envy and the men who, however much her innate modesty might want to hide it from herself, were equally envious of her companion – what was the point of worrying about that? And she let it go. Simply put the nerves and the anxieties out of her mind. She smiled at Payne and there was no way for him to know that the smile was because she had just caught herself using the words "her innate modesty". A young woman who soon will be luxuriating naked in the gaze of a lover she has never seen before has the impertinence to describe herself as innately modest! The smile turned in a moment into a laugh and it was the right thing to do, because that expression on Payne's face was one of enchantment. She had never seen it before, at any rate on someone looking at her. She was familiar with it only from romantic movies. Then she remembered how Desmond Payne made his living and the smile only intensified.

Well, the emotion on his face was genuine or it was acted. It did not matter either way. What did matter was that she was now completely relaxed, ready to enjoy the meal, the conversation, the envy of the women who watched her – and what would come later.

And the meal and conversation did prove eminently enjoyable. Desmond Payne had a fund of stories about other Hollywood luminaries and if she sometimes felt like the audience in a chat show that did not prevent her from laughing through three courses and quite a lot of the red Bordeaux that Payne had chosen to follow the champagne. At last came the moment that had never been entirely out of her mind.

'Thank you for a lovely meal,' she said. 'What happens now? I mean, I know what happens now, but how do you want to play it?'

Payne responded with a calm look that said he had done this many times before. 'I need to give my public,' and he gave a little downward turn of the lips to show that he was not entirely serious about this, 'a chance to say hello. And we go through the pantomime of your departure so that people will think we are going to separate beds. In a moment, I'll stand up. Then you will stand, I'll kiss you on the cheek and you'll leave. Eloise will be waiting for you and she will deliver you to my room by the back stairs. It's a nice room, but the reason I'm in it and not some other is that it's at the end of a corridor and round a corner so no one will see you. I'm sorry, but that is the only way to do this without getting half the Press in Europe congregating outside our door. While you're doing that, I'll be in the bar enjoying a brandy and chatting to anyone who wants to speak to me. I'll join you as fast as I can but it may be half an hour and I'll only manage that by telling people how tired I am. You'll find there's a bottle of good champagne in an ice bucket in the room; help yourself. If you want to take a shower, feel free. If you want to take your clothes off and get into bed, ditto.'

'Got it.'

He stood up, Pearl stood with him and he kissed her chastely on the cheek. In a voice loud enough for other diners to hear, Pearl said, 'It's been a lovely evening. Thank you. Dad is sure to call me tomorrow – do you have any message for him?'

Speaking at a similar volume, Payne said, 'Tell him he owes me a letter. I'll accept an email. Even a tweet will be better than nothing.'

'Dad doesn't tweet,' Pearl laughed. 'But I'll see that he gets the message. Thank you again.' And, confident that the show they had put on would fool anyone, she walked out of the dining room aware of envious heads following as she went.

She understood what Payne had meant when she reached his bedroom, for Eloise had taken her there by what was obviously a fire escape and it would have been impossible for anyone to see them on their way there. She poured herself a glass of champagne and then went into the bathroom. She wasn't going to take a shower or undress and get into bed as he had suggested she might and she knew the reason: she wanted Payne to undress her. By the end of dinner she had been on fire with lust. Her veins raged with wild and sexy hormones. Even with Uncle Martin that first time, she had never felt this level of desire. She did, however, want the experience to be as pleasant for him as it could be and so she filled the bidet with warm water, washed and dried her intimate places and then put on the clean (and delicate) knickers that she had placed in her bag just before leaving college. She sat down to wait.

It was half an hour before Desmond Payne arrived and by then Pearl had drunk a second glass of champagne and was in an even higher state of sexual excitement than when she first entered the room. Payne took the empty glass out of her hand, placed it on a table and pulled her out of the chair. The kiss he gave her now had nothing in common with the chaste peck with which they had said goodbye earlier in the dining room. When she felt his tongue pressing against her lips her mouth opened as though she would swallow it whole.

Payne stood back, took a brown envelope from his pocket and dropped it on her handbag. Realising what it must be, Pearl choked back a laugh – she, as well brought up a young woman as had ever been in this hotel, was about to sell her body for money and the idea delighted her. In truth, she had not known herself until this moment. Payne threw his jacket over a chair before taking her hands in his and holding her away from him. 'Let's have a look at you.'

She stood motionless as his eyes went the length of her body from the top of her head to her feet – she had taken off her shoes the moment she came into the room. Then, with a strength that made nothing of the task, he turned her round so that her back was to him, picked her up by the waist and threw her face down on the bed. She had no time to react before he was on the bed with her, lifting her skirt to her waist and sitting on the backs of her thighs so that she could not move. She felt his hands on her knickers and then they were simply torn from her to hang uselessly around a thigh.

'Desmond! Those are my best!'

But he was taking no notice. The weight lifted as he rose from her and she heard the sounds that said he was stripping off his clothes. Then he was back, pushing her knees apart and raising her by the hips so that, kneeling, she took her weight on her elbows. He took hold of her wrist and guided her hand to a manhood hard as iron and almost frightening in its size but there was no time for fear at what was about to possess her as he whispered, 'Put me inside you.'

For one giddy moment, Pearl thought of saying, "Say please," but that idea was banished immediately. She looked over her shoulder as she brought that magnificent missile to its target and was astonished by the ease with which it slipped into her. She had known she was ready but this was beyond all imagining. Now Payne took charge, holding her by the hips as he rode her with a vigour even greater than she had experienced with Uncle Martin. And all the time, as he took her, the ruined knickers slipped further down her thigh.

His urgency was clear in the hoarse gasps and she thought it would be over in seconds but she was in the hands of a sexual master. On he went, and on and she felt that she would collapse beneath him but his grip prevented it. He kissed her on the back of the neck; his lips nibbled at the lobe of her ear; one hand lifted from her hips long enough to smack her bottom once – twice – three times; and still the passionate probing of her sex continued. She pressed her face into the pillow to suppress the sound of her own maddened climax – and then, suddenly, his hot seed filled her and they sank into the mattress together. Pearl's warm, pink cheek was smothered in his kisses as, slowly, the great weapon on which she had been speared softened and reduced in size and he slipped out of her. His hand gently stroked her bottom. They fell asleep.

When she woke, she was still beneath him. She turned in his arms and he kissed her gently on the lips. 'Do you think it's time you took your clothes off?'

She sat up and removed her blouse and her brassiere but she had to stand to get the skirt off. She removed the torn knickers from where they had slipped to her ankle and held them in front of him. 'What am I to do with these?'

'Panties will always be a consumable item.'

'So I'd better bring extra pairs if I see you again?'

'Oh, you'll see me again. That is – if you want to?'

It had not occurred to her till now that so masculine a man – if alpha male meant anything, it meant Desmond Payne – could have doubts on that score. There were things about men that she had not yet learned. The education was something she looked forward to. 'After a performance like that, I couldn't keep away.'

He smiled and held out his arms. 'Let me hold you.'

As she snuggled against him, she realised that he was ready once more for the evidence was hard against her. She put down a hand and held it tenderly.

'How do you feel about taking it in your mouth?'

Actions speak louder than words and Pearl's only answer was to slide down the bed and do as he asked. She had done this with Uncle Martin but Uncle Martin was no match for Payne in size. Still, she took as much as she could, and under the ministrations of her tongue he seemed to grow even larger. His urgency returned; putting his hands under her arms he raised her into the air and positioned her over him. 'Impale yourself.'

Pearl reached down, held him upright in one hand and lowered herself until she felt him pressing into her. She allowed herself to go all the way down. She could not have imagined being filled so totally. Payne lay still and the message was clear: he had ridden her and now she should ride him. She began to move, and as she moved she clenched and unclenched the muscles that held him tight. She looked down at his face and saw only delight. Had she been able to look at her own face she was sure she would have seen the same thing, for now and for the first time ever with a man she was in control. They made love at her speed; the lengths he gave were measured by her. His hands slid up her body to possess her breasts, his rough palms rubbed over her taut, erect nipples. When the climax came upon her the muscles of her sex tightened and it seemed that that was too much for him because he came immediately. Keeping him in position, she lowered her head so that her long hair fell on both sides of his face as their noses touched. She kissed him.

She felt later that the night had ended too soon. They had fallen asleep once more and then been woken by the ringing of the telephone. When Pearl looked at the clock she saw that it was five thirty in the morning. Desmond Payne had answered the phone and when he put it down he said, 'I'm sorry, my love. That was Eloise. The driver is waiting and she thinks this is the time you should go.' Pearl had kissed him on the lips, dressed, kissed him again and gone downstairs. Ten minutes later, she stepped out of the car and walked past the porter's lodge.

A porter was there and awake. 'Times have changed,' he said. 'Your mother couldn't have come back at this time when she was here. She'd have been rusticated.'

'You're right,' said Pearl. 'Times *have* changed. My mother was never here because in her day people thought education was wasted on a girl. She was only going to grow up and get married and have children, so what was the point? And *that* is the change I'm interested in.'

She felt regret as she walked away from the lodge and towards her room. He had only been making conversation. He hadn't meant anything unpleasant. But Pearl was aware of the opportunities her generation had that had been denied to their mothers and it was not a point she felt able to pass by. She also knew that many – perhaps most – of the Brethren still believed that educating women beyond the point where they could read the Bible and perform enough arithmetic to manage household finances was a waste. Her dislike for the church in which she had grown up intensified.

In her room she changed quickly into clothes more suitable for a Sunday morning in college. When she opened her bag she saw the brown envelope. She flicked it open. Ten notes.

What would you call that colour? Was it pink? Or a shade of purple? In any case, each of those notes was worth fifty pounds. She would take them to the bank tomorrow, deposit nine and have the other broken into tens. She'd been brought up to understand the value of money; there weren't many occasions when she spent a whole fifty pounds in one go.

And what was this? Tucked into the bag were another five fifty pound notes. At some point during the night, presumably when she was asleep, that lovely man had given her a bonus! It was an affirming gesture – one that told her just how good she had been.

She went to breakfast as she had been instructed. After the meal she had eaten the night before she would have expected not to be hungry but in fact she felt ravenous and helped herself to poached egg on toast and three rashers of bacon as well as coffee. She had just finished when she heard the beeping that said a message had arrived on her mobile phone. Turning to shield the screen from the two girls who had joined her at the table, she read a message from Evelyn. *Want to meet?*

Sure, she replied and got another message naming a coffee shop and suggesting ten thirty that morning as a suitable time. She texted back that those arrangements suited her. Then she turned to join in the conversation with the other girls but her mind was elsewhere. What consumed her most was the memory of her second coupling with Desmond Payne – the one in which she had been on top. In control. That had been a wonderful feeling and she wanted more of it.

And so it was that she found herself at ten o'clock passing the porter's lodge once again, but this time in the opposite direction. A different porter was in charge and she returned his smile. The world felt like a wonderful place.

Evelyn and Sandra were already at the coffee shop when she arrived and both looked up in concerned expectation. 'How did it go?' asked Evelyn.

'Are you okay?' added Sandra.

'I'm fine. It went perfectly – couldn't have been better.'

The relief on both faces was clear. 'I said Desmond would be good for you,' said Sandra.

Evelyn said, 'She's had the pleasure too. She said he'd be a good one to start on.'

Sandra said, 'The thing about Desmond, he cares about the person he's with as much as his own pleasure.'

'That isn't true of everyone?'

The two women were both shaking their heads. 'I wish it were,' said Evelyn. 'Sometimes you can tell, they think they've paid for you and they treat you like a servant.'

'There's never any violence,' said Sandra, 'because that would go against everything this agency stands for and the man would never be paired with another woman.'

'In fact,' said Evelyn, 'action would be taken against him. Still, it's nice when they want you to enjoy yourself as well as them.'

Chapter 6

It might be expected that Pearl would have no place in her mind now for thoughts of anything but sex. In fact, the opposite was true. Sex matters to a young woman of eighteen but it only takes over her life if her needs are not being met and that was certainly not true for Pearl. Over the next few weeks, she had dinner with a number of men and went to bed with them afterwards. Not all were as accomplished as Desmond Payne, but none left her unsatisfied.

Some of the men she met, though, showed her how sheltered her life had been.

Marcus was a Captain of Industry. She knew that because he told her so almost as soon as they met and the capital C and capital I were implicit in the way he spoke the words. They dined at Marianne's and then a car with darkened windows conveyed them to Belton Hall, the country house hotel outside town that Evelyn had mentioned that first evening. When they got to their room, Marcus had opened his bag and taken out a short and cruel looking whip. Pearl gasped. 'I'm sorry but you're not using that on me.'

'Of course not, my dear. *You* are to use it on *me.*'

He had spread out on the bed one of the big bath towels and then lain down on it but spatters of his blood had still found their way onto the sheets. Try as she would, Pearl was unable to suppress feelings of disgust (and, she had to admit, contempt) but once he had been whipped to his satisfaction he had proved a remarkably competent lover and she congratulated herself on the professionalism with which she had handled the matter.

Jerome also brought something with him; something she would see again some weeks later. There was a harness designed to go around the waist. On one side was a dildo (she didn't know the word until he told her what it was called but the purpose was obvious) big enough that no man need feel embarrassed to have such an appendage; there was another on the other side (and pointing in the opposite direction) that was no thicker than Jerome's middle finger but was almost three times as long. Since the harness was graced with two dildos and only she possessed the kind of orifice in which such things are usually disposed, Pearl wondered how on earth the thing was meant to be used. The question was soon answered. Jerome explained that the thicker of the two erections was to fit into her. That done, he fastened the harness around her waist. Then he spread K-Y Jelly liberally over the long, thin projection. Finally he handed her the blue K-Y tube and lay face down on the bed. 'Work as much of this into my bottom as you can. Then push this little fellow into me,' and he patted the dildo affectionately. 'I'll tell you when to stop.'

Perhaps the most informative aspect of that encounter for Pearl was the sheer enjoyment she got from ramming into a man who could not resist. The thing inside her was big enough and rough enough that energetic movement brought her swiftly to orgasm but she felt no inclination to stop. Even when it was obvious that Jerome's own climax had come and gone, and until he had said several times, 'All right, dear, that's enough,' she continued to pound into him. When she finally pulled out and unhooked herself from the harness, Jerome lay on top of the bed for some time murmuring, 'Oh, God. Oh, God.' At last he stood up. 'My dear. That was the best ever. You must accept a bonus.'

What her feelings said about her attitude to sex, men and being in control she did not like to think.

Shortly after that, Pearl was sent on her first weekend assignment. She packed a variety of clothes because she could not be sure which would be appropriate. She made sure the suitcase had wheels because she knew she had to take it some little distance before being picked up. So far as anyone watching was concerned, an undergraduate hauling a bag out of the grounds was simply one more student going away for the weekend. No one noticed that she turned off three streets before the station to find the place where her "date" was waiting in his car. The car turned out to be a Bentley and a uniformed chauffeur took her bag from her before holding the back door open so that she could slide in beside the owner.

She had been told only that he was Spanish and powerful and that his name was Miguel. What she saw beside her now on the Bentley's comfortable seat was a man in his fifties, jowly, carrying more weight than was probably healthy. He took her hand in his and kissed it.

Miguel, if that was his name, proved to have perfect Castilian manners. He proved to have a wife, too. Pearl suspected that that was probably true of at least two thirds of the men she escorted but Miguel turned out to be different in that he was not inclined to be unfaithful. What he wanted was not to be the only solitary man on a working weekend. He slept in the same bed as Pearl because that was the only bed in the suite he had booked. Whether or not he was physically attracted by the slim body in the attractive negligee who took her place beside him, she had no idea. He kissed her chastely on the cheek, turned over and was soon fast asleep.

Other than that, the weekend followed what Pearl would soon recognise as the normal weekend routine. On the first afternoon, she spent time in the luxurious spa while he attended meetings. Dinner that evening for twenty people in an equally well appointed private dining room. The following morning was theirs to spend as they wished; lunch in the same private dining room with the other delegates and their wives and partners; an afternoon in which various activities were offered – Miguel and Pearl explored the local hillsides together – another dinner and another celibate night. Next morning a communal breakfast and then all departed. The driver dropped Miguel at a station from which he could take a train to Paddington and then drove Pearl to within half a mile of her lodgings.

On the second evening, just before they undressed for bed, Miguel set the timer on what looked like an expensive camera and photographed himself standing side-by-side with Pearl.

'For my wife,' he explained. 'So that she can see the beautiful girl I spent the weekend with.'

'She knows?'

'Of course she knows. She also knows that she is the only woman I love and the only woman with whom I *make* love. She trusts me. Trust between husband and wife is very important. Once it's gone you can never get it back.'

Pearl's heart warmed to this nice man. When he took the customary envelope from his pocket and handed it to her she warmed even more. 'But you haven't – you haven't *had* me.'

'I've had your time, dear girl. And I want you to know that I have enjoyed it. Any time you want to give up this life and take an honest job, call me.' And with that he handed her his card.

Of course, Pearl knew that those words "an honest job" should sting, but what was she to say? Was the life she was leading honest? She knew the answer to that.

More weekends followed, though that was the only chaste one, and Pearl came to know most of the five-star hotels in Britain. She also learned more about food and wine than anyone of her age and background could have been expected to know. Then came a date that was so important to the husband and wife team they worked for that Evelyn met her to prepare her for it. 'He's eighteen, Pearl, and a Viscount. When his father dies, he will inherit an even more senior title; one that has existed in English nobility for more than five hundred years. He'll also inherit one of the most impressive homes in the country and that is where your date will take place. His upbringing so far has been what you would expect of someone so wealthy and high born but it has lacked one important element – girls.

He should have gone up to Cambridge a term ago; these aristocrats get all sorts of privileges that aren't given to the likes of you and me. Before he goes, his parents want him to learn what a discreet and skilful woman can teach him. You'll be welcomed as a family guest, you will eat with them and when you go to bed it will be with him. His father is convinced that Angus has never so much as touched a woman and certainly he has never seen one naked. Be gentle with him.'

It was a Rolls-Royce that collected her and, though she had not thought about it, she realised she would have expected nothing else. The house was everything Evelyn had suggested it would be and Pearl was welcomed as an old family friend. Lady X (the level of discretion called for was so great that she cannot be named here and, indeed, the Viscount's name was not Angus) went with Pearl to the room she had been assigned, though she was not expected to sleep there, to say some things she wished to convey. It was an insight for Pearl into relations between aristocracy and servants that she was not inhibited from saying them in the presence of the maid who was unpacking Pearl's bag and hanging up her clothes. 'I'm afraid Angus is very nervous about what is to come. You will need to set him at his ease. There are many racy girls in our set who know how to look after themselves and still have a good time but, for whatever reason, Angus has never responded to their invitations. You may have your work cut out but I really would like to think that, by the time you leave, he will at the very least understand what goes where between man and woman.'

'You say he's nervous – is he opposed to the idea?'

'No, my dear. In fact, he has been in a state of some excitement since his father explained to him the arrangements we were making for his initiation. The problem is that Angus is shy. Shyness is something one almost never encounters among the British aristocracy and it is time he shed it. Tonight will be the first step in that process. Perhaps if he'd had sisters or brothers – sadly we were given no child but him.' She pressed an envelope into Pearl's hand. 'That is twice what we were told was the normal rate for a weekend. We expect great things from you. Let me show you his room. During dinner, Sarah,' and here she waved a hand in the direction of the maid, 'will transfer your night attire and whatever you would like to have available to put on in the morning from here to there. Angus has been told that when you retire he is to wait not less than thirty minutes before joining you, however eager he may be.'

'And in the morning?'

'You must do whatever seems fitting. But the grounds are extensive, there is a summerhouse by the lake in which we have set up a bed and placed a refrigerator with champagne and other things and I hope that matters will have gone well enough that Angus will wish to spend time there with you. The staff have been instructed to stay away unless you use the telephone to signal that you would like to take lunch there. In any case, you will find them utterly discreet.'

Pearl met Angus himself for the first time over a martini and she sat beside him at dinner. She could see that his nervousness had not been exaggerated and she rushed to quell the protective, maternal feelings it aroused in her – maternal was the last thing you wanted to feel towards someone you were about to go to bed with.

She had feared that dinner in such an august house might be a starched and formal occasion but in fact it was one of the most enjoyable meals she had eaten. Everyone at the table had been to a good school and most to a good university. They had travelled the world, knew about art, literature and history and the wit was quick. She thought, too, that Angus was overcoming his shyness as he came to know her. There were moments during their conversation when his eyes were only for her and it seemed that they moved into a sort of cocoon from which the other diners were excluded – but then the general vivacity and sociability drew them back. It seemed like no time at all before the ladies were heading for the drawing room, leaving the men to their cigars and port or brandy. 'But don't worry about that, my dear,' said Lady X. 'You can have anything you like where we are going.'

'Actually,' said Pearl, 'I think if you don't mind I'm about ready for bed. Would you mind if I retired now?' She cast a glance at Angus as she left the room. Was that anticipation she saw in his eyes? Or something even keener than that? She rather thought it might be.

She went to Angus's room as instructed, where she showered and changed into an exquisite negligee that had cost her as much as she was earning for this weekend. She still thought of herself as a frugal person who did not spend money she did not need to spend, but she had accepted that some things were necessary – and she loved the feel of this silk and lace on her bare flesh. Over the negligee she put on a belted silk dressing gown.

If Angus had been told to wait thirty minutes before joining her, he certainly waited no longer than that because Pearl was just emerging from the bathroom as he came through the door. He stopped dead and stared at her, his mouth a perfect "O". 'Pearl,' he stuttered. 'I…'

Pearl placed her hand on his chest. 'Angus. Please. Don't trip over your tongue. I have other plans for it.' She kissed him on the cheek, then stepped back holding both his hands in hers. 'You like what you see?'

'Oh, Pearl. You are perfect.'

'Thank you. And you are a sweetie. Why don't you do whatever you have to do in there,' pointing at the bathroom, 'and then…would you like to undress me?'

'Oh, I would, Pearl. I would,'

'I'll be here. Waiting.'

Angus was a young man on the verge of adulthood, well educated and heir to one of the most illustrious names in Europe – and yet, when he came to Pearl in his pyjama pants and nothing else he seemed almost like a child. As he loosened the belt and opened her gown, he reminded her of nothing so much as a young boy unwrapping a longed-for Christmas present. She let the gown slip down her arms onto the floor and lay back on the bed. When she bent one knee and put her hands behind her head, she was aware that he was looking at something that according to his father he had never seen before. She said, 'There are buttons, darling. Little pearl buttons, named after me. See?'

His fingers when they began to open the negligee were soft and gentle. Pearl said, 'Do you think you might kiss me while you're doing that?' She pressed her tongue against his lips and it took him a moment to realise that his own lips needed to open. It seemed his father's appraisal of his experience was right; he was a stranger even to kissing a girl.

Since she began working as an escort, Pearl had been fondled in almost every way she could imagine. Some of the men she had been with had been gentle and considerate and some had been abrupt but none had placed their hands on her breasts with the sweetness she experienced after Angus had undone the last button and laid her negligee open. It was as though he was experiencing a level of admiring pleasure that neither he as giver nor she as receiver had ever known. And the kissing – warm and loving – continued throughout.

It wasn't only the kissing that was warm – Pearl was feeling an excitement that had become less common as her escort work had continued. She said, 'You could start your way down now, darling.'

'Down?'

'Down. That lovely kissing you do so beautifully could move to my breasts. A little bit of sucking there wouldn't come amiss, either.' She made tiptoeing movements with her fingers down to her navel. 'And then, although don't rush it, my sweet, to here. And then,' and the fingers moved down again, 'to this place here. And when you reach there, the sucking should turn to licking.' She almost laughed at herself but didn't because she was afraid of the effect laughter might have on what was clearly as yet a fragile ego. And was she not, after all, here as a teacher?

'Oh! Oh, can I really?' And he demonstrated the answer to his own question as he drew first one breast and then the other into his mouth, sucking and at the same time running his rough tongue over the nipples in a way that had Pearl raising her bottom from the bed in anticipation of delights to come. And then down, pausing to kiss the navel, and down again, and down – and then he stopped. Pearl raised her head and saw that he was motionless an inch from the vulva that longed for contact but at which he was simply staring. 'Oh, Pearl! That is so beautiful. Oh, how I *wish* I had one of those.'

What? What was he saying? What could that possibly be

about? But that was for later. She placed a hand on the back of his head and guided him gently forwards. 'Kiss it, my pet.'

'Oh, yes, *please*.' And he did. Pearl was alive as almost never before, her nerves tingling in the ache for release.

'Your tongue, Angus. Use your tongue.'

She lay back again as the young man pleasured her but it was no good; she was on the verge of the most extraordinary climax she had ever known. She lifted her head once more. 'Take a good look, darling. At the very top. Do you see?'

'There's a sort of – I don't know what to call it. What do you call it?'

'It's a clitoris, my love. But I call it the seat of all desire. If you attend to it, if you kiss it and lick it and suck it, it will get bigger. And I will be in heaven. Would you like to be the man who took me to heaven?'

There was no answer to that question because the attention – the kissing and licking and sucking – had begun. Pearl would have liked, for Angus's sake if not for hers, to prolong this vital lesson in satisfying a woman but it was no good; she wrapped her thighs around Angus's head, holding him tight until with earth-shattering convulsions she came.

Angus raised himself to his knees and looked at her. He put both hands to his face. 'I'm spattered with your juices,' he gasped.

'Oh, darling, I'm so sorry. I was carried away.'

'Sorry! Please don't be sorry. That was the most wonderful thing I have ever known.'

Pearl raised herself with difficulty to a sitting position. She patted the place beside her. 'Lie down here beside me, my love. And take off those pyjama bottoms.'

He did as he was told. Pearl looked down at his smiling face. She kissed him on the lips. 'That's me,' she said. 'That's the taste of me.'

'You taste wonderful,' he said.

She knelt over him. Now it was her turn to work her way down. From kissing him on the lips she went on to his chest, to his stomach and then to one of the most delightful cocks she had ever looked upon. When she took the tip into her mouth, he gasped. 'Oh, Pearl! Oh, darling!' She began to work on him, her fingers on his so vulnerable sac and her mouth and her tongue running the length of that beautiful penis. It could not last and it did not. His hips rose from the bed, he gave a shudder and her mouth was filled with the salty flow of his seed. 'Oh, Pearl. Oh, I'm so sorry.'

'Sorry? Why are we both being sorry for things we should be proud of? That was what I wanted you to do.'

'It was?'

'It was.' She lay beside him and folded him into her arms. 'Darling. In a little while, we are going to make love. That means you are going to put your wonderful cock into me and I am going to give myself to you with all the affection I have. If we had done it straight away, it would have been over in seconds – just as it was a few moments ago when you came in my mouth. But now you will last much longer and you will satisfy me like the man you are. And I hope I will satisfy you like the woman I am.'

'But I was hard before and now I'm soft. How can I possibly put this into you?'

'Oh, my precious one, you'll be hard again before you know it. Wait and see.' She put her face close to his and looked into his eyes. 'When you were looking at me – down there – I don't know what words you've heard for it but that was my vulva – what did you mean when you said you wished you could have one of those?'

Angus was bright red. The shyness had returned.

Pearl said, 'We don't have to talk about this if you'd rather not. But I would like to know.' She put a hand on his cheek and kissed him gently.

'It's this stupid dream I've had since I was about twelve years old.'

'That you were a girl?'

'Well…perhaps not that. If I were a girl I couldn't inherit the title and because Mother and Pa have no other children, the line would pass to my cousin. And my parents don't like my cousin and neither do I. He was horrid to me at Harrow.'

'Horrid in what way?'

Angus looked away. 'He called me a tart. You know – a girl. Because I was no good at rugger. I always enjoyed cricket and I was in the First Eleven but he said cricket was a tart's game, a game for sissies, and not something that real men would bother with.'

'Well, Angus, let me tell you something. The pleasure you gave me a few moments ago, only a real man could give.' She looked down. 'And look. Didn't I tell you you'd be hard again before you knew it? It takes a real man to have one of those and it takes a real man to use it to bring pleasure to a woman. Now I'm going to lie down and you are going to lift yourself over me and I am going to guide you into me and you, my love, are going to give me a damn good fucking. A real man's fucking.'

Because he had so recently emptied himself into Pearl's mouth, Angus was able to go on for a long time. For a young man making love to a woman for the first time he gave a most creditable account of himself and when he emptied himself a second time, and this time into Pearl's vagina, the look on his face said that his sense of self-worth had risen dramatically. They lay face to face and hugged each other.

The silence between them was broken only by contented breathing and the smack of occasional kisses. Then Angus said, 'Do you really think I'm a real man?'

'Well, my darling. Do you think I'm a real woman?'

Angus breathed out in astonishment. 'Oh, yes. You're the most wonderful woman I could ever have imagined.'

'And you just satisfied me. Totally. So what does that make you?'

He smiled. 'I'm so glad you're here. So glad it's you. Mother said I'd like you but she didn't say how much.'

'I think it's probably a good idea if we go to sleep now,' said Pearl. 'We'll both still be here in the morning and you can be a real man and I can be a real woman all over again. There's just one thing.' She got up and went to the clothes that the

maid Sarah had left for her to choose from next day. As she
had hoped – indeed, as she had instructed because she had
not known what the morning would bring – there were three
pairs of knickers in different styles. She picked up the pair that
she thought would most suit the moment. Back at the bed,
she dropped them on the pillow beside Angus's head. 'This is
entirely up to you. You don't have to do anything you don't
feel comfortable with. But you talked about the wishes you
sometimes had and if you felt you wanted to sleep tonight
in those instead of your pyjamas then you can do so. Or, of
course, you can sleep in nothing at all.'

'Oh!' He looked at her doubtfully. 'We'd never be able to
tell my parents I wore these. They must never know about
something like that.'

'They won't hear from me. You can be quite sure of that.'

When she fell asleep shortly afterwards, the knickers were
still on the pillow beside Angus's head. But when she woke
at two in the morning he was wearing them.

Tomorrow is another day, but you would not have known that
had you been in Angus's bedroom when they woke because the
activities at five in the morning were much as they had been
the previous evening – though Angus took a more active role,
for what brought Pearl to consciousness was the realisation
that someone was kissing her between the legs.

'Darling,' she said, pushing his head away. 'I need to use
the bathroom.' When she was on her feet she held out a hand.
'Come and watch.'

He needed no encouragement and knelt on the floor to
watch as her water tinkled into the bowl. She said, 'Darling,
you need to know that not all women will be happy for you
to watch them do this. You are born and raised to be a gentleman and something no gentleman ever does is to impose on
a woman something she does not like. And I can tell you that
there are some things I might be doing here where I would
not want you present.'

'It would be good if there were rules saying what we may

and may not do.'

'Good, perhaps, but impossible. The whole business varies so much. It might even be that every single individual in the world is different in what they like and don't like and what they will and will not do. I think happiness between men and women only comes when they are in tune with each other; when each knows the other's preferences and respects them. But some things should be universal. Like this.' And she moved from lavatory bowl to bidet, poured water into it and sponged herself clean. 'I will taste much nicer to you now. And, my darling, you should know that any woman will be happier to take into her mouth a man who has been careful to clean himself there than one who has not.'

'Oh. I see.' And Angus refilled the bidet and washed his penis. Pearl was tempted to say, 'Good boy,' but they were not yet at a point where she could rely on his ability to be teased. She took his hand once more and led him back to the bed. 'What would you most like to do now?'

'If I could do anything?'

She nodded.

'Well, if I could do anything, what I would really like to do is – what do you call it, that thing where I use my tongue on your – well. And what you call *that*?'

Pearl smiled. 'There are many things you can say. I've heard it called muff diving, though I'm not sure I'm terribly happy with that. The Latin word is cunnilingus but probably most English people would say you were eating me out or going down on me. As for what you call this,' and she placed his hand between her legs, 'well, once again there are Latin words. This is my vulva and this,' extending one of his fingers so that she could put it into herself, 'is my vagina. But if you like you can call it my fanny or my cunt or many other words. Though I suggest you don't use the word cunt anywhere where your mother could hear you. In fact, you should never use it to a woman unless you love each other and you say it in an intimate and affectionate way with no one else around to hear.'

'Well,' said Angus. 'In that case what I should most like

would be to eat your cunt until I hear that lovely suppressed scream you gave last night because that said how much you were enjoying it and then I should like to put myself into you.'

'To fuck me.'

'To fuck you. Although I think that's another word I had better not use in public.'

Pearl lay back and spread her legs, bending the knees. 'That sounds like a wonderful idea to me. And while you're eating me out and paying special attention to…'

'…to your clitoris…'

'…to my clitoris or my clitty or my clit or my little nubbin…'

'…so many lovely words for such lovely things…'

'…while you're doing that, you can give me even greater pleasure by putting your finger into my cunt and moving it in and out. Actually there is something even more wonderful for a woman than that but I don't know that we are quite ready for that lesson.'

'Perhaps later?'

'Perhaps later. Would you like to start?'

He would. He did. And when Pearl had had her orgasm and then given him the words for it, he entered her once again with his delightful penis and had an orgasm all of his own. Then they went back to sleep and did not wake until nine o'clock at which time the noises of the house were all around them.

No one commented on how late they were to breakfast, though from the expression on Lady X's face, Pearl believed that she was pleased. She could not have failed to see how happy her son looked. Pearl and Angus were the last to arrive in the dining room and it was empty when they had finished. Pearl said, 'What would you like to do this morning?' and laughed when she saw the lustful expression that came onto his face. 'Perhaps I should have said, *where* would you like to do what you'd like to do this morning?'

Angus looked puzzled, as though the only place for what he wanted to do was the place where they'd already done it – his bedroom. Pearl said, 'Your mother mentioned a summerhouse by the lake. Apparently there's a bed there.'

'Oh, yes. The summerhouse.'

'And the staff have been told to stay away. Unless we want to have lunch there, in which case she says we have to phone for it. I never encountered a summerhouse with its own phone before.' Angus looked puzzled once more and Pearl guessed that he could not imagine a summerhouse without one. 'So,' she said. 'Do you want to show me the summerhouse?'

'That's why you dressed like that, isn't it? The shorts and that lovely cotton – what? What is it?'

'Dear me, Angus, there are an awful lot of words you don't know and they all relate to girl things. You can call it a top or you can call it a blouse or I suppose you could even call it a shirt. I chose it because it has buttons, and so do the shorts, and you've shown yourself to be rather good with buttons. Now stop evading the question. Do you want to show me the summerhouse?'

'Yes, Pearl. I can't think of anything I'd rather do than show you the summerhouse.'

'I know you can think of one thing you'd rather do. But it's okay because we can do it in the summerhouse. Let's go to your room first.'

When they got there, Pearl was astonished by how quickly the room had been tidied. Her negligee was neatly folded and placed on one pillow; the knickers Angus had worn during the night were on the other. Pearl pointed wordlessly at them, but Angus was unconcerned. 'It's all right for Sarah to know. Maids know everything. She won't tell my parents.'

'What have you got on under those lovely white slacks that probably cost as much as my father spends on clothes in six months?'

Angus unzipped his pants and held them wide to show a pair of equally white boxer shorts. 'Well,' Pearl said, 'those are lovely and they'll do just fine. Unless you'd like to spend the day in these?' And she held up the third, so far unworn pair of knickers. 'These are called French Knickers and they have these lovely little legs that a person can put a hand up. This is called broderie anglaise. Aren't they sweet?'

'They are. But if one can put a hand up the leg, they might be better on you.'

Quick as a flash, Pearl removed her shorts, dropped on the floor the pretty panties she had put on that morning and donned the French Knickers. Then she put her shorts back on. 'If you have hand-up-leg ambitions, we'll go to my room first and I'll change into a nice short skirt. What are you doing?' Because Angus was removing his slacks and his boxer shorts and picking up the panties Pearl had dropped. 'Oh. Yes. I see what you're doing. A great idea.'

After they had been to Pearl's room so that she could change into a skirt, they walked hand in hand to the summerhouse. They could have got there in ten minutes but in fact it took forty because Angus wanted to show Pearl something of the grounds. 'Are there fish in that lake?' asked Pearl.

'Of course there are fish in the lake,' said Angus in a voice that suggested a lake without fish was unthinkable.

The summerhouse was to the summer houses that Pearl knew as Windsor Castle is to a children's tree fort. She had pictured the bed occupying almost the whole of the floor and making it difficult to open and close the door. In fact, it was in a separate room from what Pearl supposed you would have to call the reception room – a reception room that was huge while the bedroom was merely large. Nor were these the only two rooms; there was a well-furnished bathroom and an equally fully equipped kitchen. The kitchen had its own external door. 'If we do phone for lunch…'

'…which we probably will…'

'…it will be brought through that door and prepared for us there.'

'And I suppose whoever brings it will knock very politely on our door and stay on the other side of it in case we are *in flagrante.*'

'Of course,' said Angus in a way that once again asked the question: what other way is there?

When they returned to it, Pearl decided that she was going to call the reception room a sitting room. It was amply furnished, with a choice of seating arrangements. Pearl selected a sofa long enough for four people and patted the seat beside her. 'This is big enough for us both to lie down on,' she said. 'Should the idea of lying down seem attractive at any point.' She put an arm round Angus's shoulder, turned his face gently towards hers and kissed him. 'Now, listen. We're both having a lovely time. At least, I am and I rather think you are too?'

'I've never known such bliss.'

'That's what I thought and I'm glad. What I want you to know is that there is no hurry. Whatever we feel like doing, we'll get there.' She listened to herself and wondered whether she was being too much the schoolmarm, but was she not after all here to teach Angus all he needed to know? 'How do the panties feel?'

Angus smiled. 'Lovely.'

'Good. You don't wish you could wear a skirt as well?'

She was getting used to the expression that said that Angus didn't understand what he was being asked – which meant, of course, that she didn't understand him. Still, understanding was drawing closer with every conversation of this sort. 'No,' he said. 'I don't want to be a girl and I don't want to look like one. But I love having something soft and feminine close to my skin. And I love the fact that people can look at me and not know that I have it there.'

'So when you said that thing about wishing you had something…something I have…'

'A cunt, Pearl. I said I wished I had a cunt. But I stopped wishing that when you showed me what I could do with yours.' His words pleased Pearl for they meant that she had delivered what Lady X had paid her for.

It wasn't, now, Pearl who was kissing Angus so much as Angus who was kissing Pearl. Watching him turning into the man his parents wanted him to be gave her great satisfaction. His hand when he placed it on her thigh was warm and gentle but there was an insistence about the way it moved towards the hem of her skirt. And then it was under the hem, and then his fingers were slipping under the leg of the French Knickers and Pearl was laying back and drawing him with her and the first of his fingers found the moist and willing lips of her sex. She was on her back now, her knees bent and apart and his fingers were in her and his thumb was on the little nubbin at the top and the little nubbin was becoming less little by the second and her hips were moving and his fingers were pushing in and out and he was over her and on top of her and his knees were between hers and her arms were wrapped around his back and her climax came and she realised that no one could hear them and that, actually, it wouldn't matter if anyone did and as she bucked beneath his hand she let the scream come out, the scream that so often she held inside.

The French called this *le petit mort* – the little death – and the description had never been more apt for Pearl than it was now as she subsided into a little oblivion. Angus was kissing her on the throat and on the cheek and on the lips and back to the throat and his hands were unbuttoning the blouse and he was removing it with no help from her and then he was grappling with the brassiere, something he had never done before and it held him for a few moments but he did it, he unclipped the brassiere and slid it from her arms, once more without her help. Then it was the turn of the skirt and then the knickers themselves and Pearl was naked and his lips and his tongue were buried between her legs and the cunt that had just been roused to uproar was roused to uproar again.

A blessed languor possessed her. Angus lay beside her, his arms around her, his lips against her cheek. 'This is meant,' he said.

She stirred gently. 'What do you mean, darling?'

'This. You and me together. Something like this does not happen by accident. We are meant to be together. I love you, Pearl.'

'Oh, Angus. You'll love so many people before you're done.'

'No! Never like this. I love you and I want to marry you.'

This was not supposed to be happening. This was not part of the deal. She was supposed to initiate him into the ways of men and women, not lead him away from the life that was laid down for him. She sat up. 'Angus. You must not say that. I'm…' She was a what? What could she say? Was she to use the word she had always shied away from in her head? She must. 'I'm a whore, Angus. I go to bed with men for money. You will meet so many lovely girls and one of them will be for you.'

She sank back and they lay in silence. Then, in a very quiet voice, he said, 'How did it happen?'

Pearl felt a dreadful weariness descend on her. 'How did what happen?'

'That word. That thing you said you are. Which I do not accept. You can't use a word like that about someone as loving and gentle as you. How did you come to be what you say you are and I say you are not?'

'Oh, Angus. It's not a nice story.'

'I want to hear it.'

Did he have the right to ask that? Of course he did not. And Pearl knew that, if she went now to Lady X and said, "I can do no more. My job is finished," then Lady X would still know that she had had her money's worth. Angus had no right to hear Pearl's story. But she felt an irresistible need to tell it.

When she was done, Angus lay without speaking but his arms were wrapped around her more tightly than ever. At last he said, 'That man – your Uncle Martin – was a swine. A disgrace. How could anyone treat someone like that? And the elders. What kind of religion are they practising? Is that what they think God's love is? And as for your mother…'

'That's enough, Angus. What I did with Uncle Martin was wrong.'

'No! What he did with *you* was too awful even to think about. But you – you did nothing wrong. You were an innocent girl and he got you drunk and you gave yourself to him as he wanted and then he dumped you. The man should be in jail.'

Now it was Pearl's time for silence which she broke when she said, 'I think I should leave.'

He tightened his grip even more. 'I want you to stay.'

'Then I will, but only if you promise to speak of this no more.'

'But…'

'No, Angus. No more.'

'Very well. But I shall not forget what those horrible people did to you.'

'Angus!'

'No more. I understand.' His tight grip on her relaxed as he snuggled close. 'You said there was something even better than what we did in the middle of the night and you said you would show me later. It's later now.'

'Darling. Give me time to get myself together.'

'You can have all the time you want. And one day you will spend that time with me.'

'I'm with you now.'

'I don't mean that. I mean together. I'm only a year younger than you. Perhaps not even that. And I know the most wonderful person I've ever met when I see her.'

In spite of herself, Pearl laughed. 'Angus, that's the most Irish thing I've heard in an age.' But she wasn't laughing in her heart. In her heart, she was moved by this young man as she had not been by any of the men she had lain with before. He would be so easy to fall in love with. And she must not do that. She must not. She would not. She sat up. 'The thing that I told you was even more wonderful than the thing we did this morning was taught to me by Uncle Martin. Do you still want to do it?'

'I do. And I want you to put all thoughts of him out of your mind.'

'Easier said than done. In my purse there, you'll find a little blue tube.' When he had found it she said, 'That's K-Y Jelly. You're going to put it on your finger and then you're going to put your finger in my bottom.'

'In your *bottom*! Oh, Pearl.'

'And then you're going to keep it there while I turn over, and then you're going to eat me out and while you're doing it your finger is going to be moving and you're going to give me the most stunning orgasm.' She kissed him. 'And then, my darling, it will be long past the time for *your* orgasm, and we're going to see that you have it. Does that sound all right?'

'It sounds wonderful.'

'Good.' She stood up. 'I think this should take place in bed.'

Pearl and Angus spent the rest of that Saturday together, not always alone as Lady X had firm expectations with regard to dinner which in this house was an occasion for everyone who was home or visiting at the time to gather, eat and talk. They were together all night and inseparable on Sunday morning. For a large part of that time, one or both of them was either very scantily dressed or had no clothes on at all. Then came the time for Pearl's departure. Lady X took her to one side – not without difficulty, given Angus's desire to be with her all the time. 'My dear, you have been so good for Angus. He is transformed. I can't thank you enough. I hope you haven't found him too much of a trial.'

'He's a wonderful young man. I've enjoyed every moment.' This did not seem the time to mention that Angus had brought her closer to tears than anyone since she had left home as he forced her to re-examine the life she was living. It was the most natural thing in the world that he should ask for her address so that he could write and her mobile number so that they could speak – but she refused. And no, she said, she had no Facebook page and she did not Tweet. Angus said, 'This has just been a commercial occasion for you,' and Pearl replied that, yes, that was exactly what it had been although she knew it was a lie. It would be a gross violation of her duty to Lady X to grant any room to the longing she felt – the feeling that this naïf and green young man was someone she could fall deeply in love with.

Angus did not cling to her in public and beg her not to leave. Five centuries of breeding did not permit such a thing. Nevertheless, the depth of Angus's feelings for Pearl was clear to the family. She wondered how such aristocrats felt about such a thing. It didn't matter; he was young, he would be going up to

Cambridge and new experiences would crowd out whatever memories he retained of this weekend. He would forget her very quickly. She hoped that the same would be true for her.

Chapter 7

When she got home from her tryst with Angus, it was impossible to go on ignoring the simple fact that it would soon be Christmas. Pearl had not been home once since she started university and she missed her family but she had come to a decision: however much she might miss them, she was not going to spend the holiday at home if any of the family (and she meant her mother) would refuse to sit at the dinner table with her.

This must also have been in her father's mind because he called her. 'Petal, I know it's difficult for you to come here so I'm coming there. We'll have dinner together and talk about the holiday.'

'Okay. When do you have in mind?'

'I'm on a business trip all week and I won't be far from you on Tuesday.'

'Tuesday's fine.'

'There's a Holiday Inn I can stay in. I've looked in the *Good Food Guide* and Marianne's sounds like a good place to eat. A bit pricey; I don't suppose student ever gets to eat there.'

Pearl smothered a giggle. 'No, I shouldn't think so.'

'I'll book a table at seven. My treat, obviously.'

Next day, though she had no client, Pearl visited Eloise. 'My father is taking me to dinner here on Tuesday.'

Eloise laughed. 'Good Heavens! Well, you can rely on us. I'll make sure all the staff know to treat you as someone they never clapped eyes on.'

'My family belongs to a strict religious sect. It's unlikely we'll drink alcohol.'

'Ouch. I see your problem.'

Pearl dressed with care for the occasion. Long skirt. Demure sweater and jacket. Flat shoes. No make up.

Her father was clearly ill at ease, but whether because of their family problems or because he was unused to such opulent surroundings Pearl could not have said. 'How are you, chick?'

'I'm fine. I love it here.' She smiled. 'I mean at uni – not this place.'

'No. I don't think I've ever seen half of the things on this menu. What are we going to eat?'

They spent the next five minutes going through the menu with Pearl deliberately choosing the most everyday (and cheapest, because this was her father and she didn't want to embarrass him) dishes. He said, 'And what would you like to drink?'

'Water,' she said in a voice that suggested no alternative occurred to her.

'Still or sparkling?' asked the waiter.

'A jug of tap water will be fine,' said Pearl.

When the waiter had gone, her father said, 'If you want a glass of wine I don't have a problem with that.'

Pearl knew that she was going to refuse to go home for Christmas and because she also knew that she would refuse an offer of money to finance her stay she had prepared a story. It did not sit easy with her to lie to her father (her mother would have been a different matter, for Pearl had not forgiven her mother's rejection) but she saw no alternative. 'I work in the college bar, Daddy. They pay me for it and I need the money. I'm in there for four hours, five evenings a week and I haven't touched a drop yet.'

Her father nodded.

'It's nothing to do with religion. It was alcohol that got me into trouble.'

'Yes. Martin turned out to be a rotter. I never speak to him these days. So. Look. We need to talk about the holiday.'

'There's only one thing I need to know. If I come home, will Mummy sit at the same table with me to eat?'

'I've talked to her…you know how strongly she holds to the elders' views.'

'So the answer is no. Then I won't be coming home.'

Her father had picked up a bread roll and was crumbling it to pieces in his hands. Pearl could see that he didn't know he was doing it. 'I was afraid you would say that.'

She put her hand on his. 'Stop torturing that poor piece of bread. It isn't that I don't love you all and miss you. But I feel angry about what happened. The choice is between having Christmas without my family or joining them but not being able to eat with them or go to church with them.'

'You know, you could ask to meet the elders. You could repent. Martin got away with that and he's far more to blame than you were.'

She took a deep breath. 'I'm not going to do that. I don't know what the future holds for me but I do know that I'm finished with the Brethren. For ever.' As she spoke the words, she felt as though a weight had been lifted from her shoulders.

'I was afraid of that, too.'

Then their first courses arrived. Her father raised his glass of water and chinked it against hers. 'You will always be my beloved daughter.'

'Yes, Daddy. I always will.'

'How will you spend Christmas?'

'I've been invited to a fellow student's home.'

'A man?'

'No, not a man.' She smiled, a smile full of sadness. 'I'm not ready for any more men.'

When she walked home that evening relief at having faced up to the Brethren was tempered by regret that she had lied to her father – about the job in the bar; about not having touched alcohol; about having nothing to do with men. She had also lied by omission in that she had said nothing about her non-academic activities. She had been brought up always to tell the truth. She had come a long way from the person she had once been and the knowledge saddened her.

When she was not working – she could not think of it as anything but working – her academic life blossomed. Not being left, as most of her fellow-students were left, wondering about the next drunken evening and the next coupling, she was free to devote herself to the study of her chosen subject.

Because she had not ruled it out, at the end of the week

in which her father had visited she found herself called to a weekend of a sort she had never really thought about.

She packed an overnight bag and carried it to the designated pickup point. When the dark blue Aston Martin drew into the curb she suppressed a nervous gulp as she looked at the driver but opened the passenger door and slid into her seat. The feeling as the car sped away was one of raw power; the feeling in her stomach was of butterflies.

The driver placed a hand on Pearl's thigh and smiled before returning her hand to the wheel and her attention to the road. 'Pearl. I'm Madeleine.' A voice no different from any other woman's (but what had she expected?) with an attractive east coast American accent. 'I'm glad you could join me. Shall I brief you before we get there?'

'Please.'

'Let's get the business part out of the way first.' She reached into the pocket at the base of the door and handed Pearl a white envelope which Pearl tucked into her handbag. 'There. Now we can forget about that and just be friends. Intimate friends.' She glanced for a moment at Pearl, who was left in no doubt; if Desmond Payne, like most of the men she had met since Evelyn and Sandra had brought her into the business, was an alpha male then Madeleine was an alpha female. Pearl wasn't sure that she had ever met such a powerful woman. 'You've been to parties before?'

'Of course. But only with men.'

'There's really very little difference. It will be a small gathering, and select. There are ten of us; women in senior positions in banking and industry who like to get together from time to time in female-only company. At any one time, some of the ten will always be out of the country and this weekend there will only be six of us. Nine, if you count the partners.'

'Not everyone will bring a partner?'

'As I said, the weekend will be restricted by gender. Some of our number are married to men or in steady relationships with them. The only partners who are welcome are female.

Here is a good place to stop.'

They were out of town now and the "good place to stop" was a layby. No one else was parked there. Madeleine brought the car to a halt and unclipped her seatbelt. She turned and leaned across to place a hand on Pearl's cheek. 'My partner and I split a few weeks ago and I don't want to turn up alone. There are appearances to be kept up. Apart from which, it will be an excellent opportunity for a romp in the hay. Not that there'll be any hay; the beds where we are going are sumptuous. You're blushing. You've really never been with a woman?'

'You're the first,' stammered Pearl.

'And you're okay with it?'

Pearl examined her feelings. She wanted to be honest with the woman. 'I'm looking forward to it. But I'm a bit nervous.'

Madeleine leaned closer and kissed her on the lips. This was a moment of truth and Pearl entered into the kiss fully. Madeleine said, 'Honey, you should have seen the state I was in the first time I accepted what I was and let a woman have me. And that was nothing compared with coming out to my parents. My father didn't take it well. He's a big deal in New York State. He's made and unmade governors and presidents. To him, a woman's job is to stand just behind her man. Host dinners for him. Be a figurehead on the boards of charities.'

'Is he okay with you now?'

Madeleine turned to the wheel, put her seatbelt on and took the car back onto the road. 'It took time. Part of the deal was that I look for a job in Europe so I wouldn't be flaunting what I am in his backyard all the time. But he's fine when I go back there for a few days. I can even take a partner with me as long as I understand that we won't be meeting any of his business associates. Anyways, back to the weekend. Not everyone will arrive in time for lunch, but we will. There'll be business meetings this afternoon but you won't be expected to attend those. There's a pool and a spa and partners usually spend their spare time being pampered.'

It really was to be very like the other parties she'd attended.

'That will be charged to my bill of course. Go down in one

of the dressing gowns hanging in our bathroom and choose whatever you want. A massage, maybe a pedicure and nail job – whatever. The other partners are likely to ask questions and I'd be grateful if you'd just stick to saying that we met a few weeks ago and became an item. Don't give any more details than that. Certainly don't say that I'm paying for your company. And the same goes with the other members.'

'You can rely on my discretion.'

'I know that, honey. It's one of the things I'm paying for.' She put her hand back on Pearl's thigh. 'After the meetings there'll be a couple hours before dinner and we can get to know each other properly. Then dinner. After that we'll have all night together. Tomorrow will be much the same but there's an understanding that there is no rush to get up in the morning for those who don't want to and no business starts until after lunch. I usually take breakfast in my room.' The hand tightened. 'Are those suspenders I can feel?'

Pearl nodded.

'Delightful. I can see I'm going to enjoy our weekend together.'

In fact, "getting to know each other properly" did not wait till the time before dinner. Pearl was conscious of a mood in Madeleine that she had seen before, but only in men. She'd have liked to think that it was affection, but she knew it was something more simple than that – it was lust. This woman wanted her, as so many men had wanted her. The expression "sex object" had never entered her mind in relation to what she had done in hotel rooms around the country, possibly because she had not allowed it to, but it was there now. The agency could have sent any of their female escorts for this weekend and Madeleine's attitude would have been the same: she would have seen them as there for her sexual gratification. She had said of Pearl's discretion, "It's one of the things I'm paying for". She was paying for other things, too, and she intended to have them.

Madeleine picked up the room service menu and ordered

lunch for them both without consulting Pearl. No man had ever done that. When it arrived – soup, a smoked salmon salad and a bottle of chardonnay – she had the waiter wheel it onto the balcony. Pearl thought it late in the year for that, and a little chilly, and she thought so even more when the waiter had gone and Madeleine said, 'I'd like to see you in your scanties,' but the customer was always right. At least the balcony was secluded; when she had stripped off her skirt, blouse and slip, no-one but Madeleine could see her. She was grateful for the warming effect of the wine.

Madeleine ate quickly and Pearl was happy to follow her example because, while it was clear that Madeleine's haste was in anticipation of what would follow, Pearl simply wanted to get off the balcony and into the warm room. When they were done, Madeleine said, 'You want to freshen up for me, honey?' Pearl went into the bathroom, did what she needed to do and then washed her lower parts in the bidet. When she came back, Madeleine had pushed the lunch trolley into the corridor, pressed the little button that turned on the Do Not Disturb light outside the door and put the safety catch in place. She had also taken off her skirt and blouse. Even half undressed, she remained the most powerful female person Pearl had ever looked at and Pearl felt in her stomach a little tremor of anticipation that was not entirely unmixed with fear.

Madeleine took her hand, pulled her into an embrace and kissed her. Her tongue invaded Pearl's mouth. Her hands moved up Pearl's back and unsnapped the brassiere, stepping back to slip it down her arms and throw it onto the floor. She looked at her prize, bringing her hands up to start the coral nipples into life. 'You really are a beauty, hun.' She kissed her again. Then, 'The panties, please.'

When the knickers lay on the floor beside the brassiere, Pearl stood in nothing but her garter belt and stockings. Madeleine's hand slid down Pearl's stomach and she began to finger the young woman's sex and Pearl held the other woman's arms as she felt the fever rising till she thought she would climax at any moment – but her mistress was not yet ready for that. She pulled back the duvet, revealing cotton sheets as luxurious as anything Pearl had experienced. 'Get into bed.'

Pearl lay on her back, watching as Madeleine took off the rest of her clothes. The woman could not be described as fat but it was a powerful body – as powerful in its way as the Aston Martin she drove. Her bush did not look like a bush that had been trimmed. Madeleine climbed onto the bed, straddled Pearl's hips and began to move forward. Once in position, she lowered herself towards Pearl's face. Pearl knew what she had enjoyed when men had used their tongues to pleasure her in this way. She had no difficulty in showing Madeleine what she had learned.

Madeleine's climax was not quick in coming and by the time it arrived Pearl had developed a sympathy for the men who had performed the same act on her. Why had they never complained that their jaws ached? And had their faces really been smeared with her juices the way hers was now by Madeleine's?

Madeleine rose from her and went to her suitcase. She placed two objects on the pillow. Pearl's stomach turned over when she saw that one was exactly the same as the one she had used on Jerome while in the other, both dildos were the same size – and that size was not small. Madeleine began to smear the long thin one with K-Y Jelly. 'Turn onto your front, hun.'

It was done with despatch and Pearl realised that Madeleine was already thinking about the meetings she had soon to attend. When she was face down, Madeleine lifted her by the hips and pushed a pillow under her and between her legs. There was a short pause as Madeleine got the harness into place, grunting in a very unfeminine way as she inserted the large dildo into her own sex, and then she parted Pearl's bottom cheeks with one hand and guided the thin dildo into her with the other. 'Now, you little strumpet. Let's give that rosebud a workout.'

Pearl's first reaction was one of affront. She was being used like a whore. Madeleine was taking her pleasure without thought for the woman she was rogering. Okay, there was enjoyment for Pearl – being penetrated by something no thicker than a finger was not like having a man there with an organ far too big for the small and sensitive place. Nevertheless, she would have liked some indication that she mattered, too.

And then the frottage kicked in.

Pearl had never experienced anything like this before. As Madeleine moved, Pearl's sex ground up and down on the pillow between her legs. She had heard of this – of women getting off on other women's thighs, on their hips or even on the pommel of a horse's saddle – but it had never happened to her and she had doubted that it could ever be truly rewarding. She realised now how wrong she had been. Her movements became more and more frenetic; she did not remember ever being quite so out of control. Madeleine's mouth was close to her ear, egging her on, goading her. 'Go, girl. Work that snatch.' None of the men Pearl had been with had ever talked dirty to her and though she felt she should have been disgusted, in fact she was as aroused as she had ever been. It was a good job the dildo was as long as it was because otherwise she was afraid that her bucking must throw Madeleine off and, whatever she wanted, she knew she did not want this to end.

Yet end it must. She climaxed with such force that she worried about what she might have done to the pillow, and seconds later a gasping shriek told her that Madeleine, too, was done. The woman subsided onto her. Then Pearl felt the weight lift and she knew that Madeleine had unhooked herself from the harness and was lying beside her – but instead of removing the dildo from Pearl's bottom, she was stroking it in a leisurely, desultory fashion. With each gentle twist, Pearl let out another soft groan.

'So,' said Madeleine. 'Now that you've had the real thing, do you want more?'

'Oh,' murmured Pearl, 'yes, please.'

'Next time it will be the Big Boy.'

'In my front bottom, I hope.'

At last, Madeleine removed the weapon with which she had so thoroughly rogered Pearl. 'Don't be so coy. We're both women together. When you mean cunt, say cunt. Turn onto your back.'

She lay on top of Pearl, kissing her on the lips. 'I have to go now, honey. Enjoy yourself in the spa. Spend whatever you want. I'll be back here about six and I will expect to be welcomed with open legs. I'll have an ice bucket and a bottle of champagne delivered.' She smacked Pearl on the hip, stood up and began to dress. Pearl found it odd that she would meet the other women without showering first but she said nothing. It did not occur to her that Madeleine might wish the others to smell the sex hanging heavy about her.

Left alone, Pearl lay in bed and considered what had just happened to her. She was tired – almost exhausted, in fact – and she looked forward to a massage simply to get back in shape for the second bout that Madeleine had told her to expect but her mind was in turmoil. She did not believe that any of the men she had been with would have dealt with her or spoken to her as Madeleine had. The woman had called her a strumpet! And she had taken her without reserve in a way that Pearl had made clear would be available to no man, simply plunging a cock substitute into Pearl's bottom without so much as a by-your-leave. Pearl felt almost obscenely used.

And yet. As a straightforward sexual act it had been at least as satisfying – as enjoyable – as *thrilling* – as anything Pearl had dreamed of, let alone experienced. She was sated as she had rarely been even with the most experienced men who had had her.

She wanted more.

There was little doubt that the masseuse knew what Pearl was at the hotel for. Her hands were skilled but they hovered on the edge of propriety. Pearl had visited spas before when the men she was with were at meetings and a massage had always been part of those visits but never had she felt – as she felt now – that her private places might be invaded.

And then the line was crossed. Pearl was already feeling restored, to physical well-being if not to a sensual balance (for she was still not entirely sure how she felt about her body being plundered by a woman) when the masseuse rolled her onto her front, threw to the floor the blanket that had covered her and knelt on the table. 'Ms Bronwy said to give you a little extra at the end of the massage.'

Ms Bronwy must be Madeleine. 'How did she know it would be you that looked after me?'

'She didn't. She gave us all the same instruction.'

So not just this masseuse but the whole staff knew Pearl's business. She felt herself growing pink. 'And the little extra?'

The masseuse giggled. 'She wants you in a state of anticipation.' And with that she began to stroke the cheeks of Pearl's bottom. Once again, Pearl's first reaction was one of indignation. How could she be expected to put up with this sort of treatment? But the stroking was seductive. The girl's hands never quite strayed far enough to make Pearl revolt; her thumbs came within a whisker of lips that were moist and straining for release but never touched what they had no right to touch. The moment to object was gone, for Pearl's excitement must be as clear to her tormentor as it was to her. Pearl could only guess where the girl had learned to excite a woman in the way that she was excited. She felt that the merest touch on her sex would bring her to shuddering orgasm. But that touch never came.

It was as though Pearl were in a trance and when it ended she heard the masseuse's voice as if from a distant cloud. 'Pearl? Pearl? It's twenty to six. Time you were back in your room. Ms Bronwy will be there soon.'

The girl had to help Pearl into her clothes. Then she said, 'I'd better walk you back. I don't think you'd make it on your own.' When they got there, she said, 'Oh, champagne! Enjoy your evening, Pearl. Oh, dear. You're still not back with us, are you? Look, take those things off.' Pearl, who seemed to have lost all conscious will, took off her clothes and dropped them on the floor. The masseuse was searching Pearl's case. She picked up a negligee – the same negligee, as it happened, that had so thrilled Angus. 'Perfect.' She turned to Pearl. 'Lift up your arms and let me get this on you. There. You look beautiful. Ms Bronwy will be delighted. Now get into bed and wait for her.' And she picked up the clothes that Pearl had dropped, folded them and placed them on an ottoman, and left the room.

Pearl did not have to wait long. Madeleine entered the room, poured two glasses of champagne and put one on each bedside table. Then she drew down the top sheet and – there was only one word that Pearl thought described what she was doing – ogled her. 'My, my. Don't you look captivating? What an adorable negligee. You really are beautiful, honey bun. I could eat you all up.' And now her smile was, to Pearl, more of a leer. 'But we don't want to get you overheated again, do we? Not till later.'

Pear felt she really had to say something. 'Madeleine...'

'Call me Maddy, honey. After what we've already done together I think a little intimacy is okay, don't you?'

'Maddy.'

'Oh, dear. You're in a snit, aren't you? Are you feeling used?'

'I know you've paid for me, but...'

'Yes, Pearl. I have. And I haven't paid for any buts. Are you going to tell me you didn't enjoy what we did earlier? Oh, my, if you could see yourself! You've gone bright pink. Shall I tell you what you're thinking?' She carried on without waiting for an answer. 'You think when you're with me it should be just like being with a man except that an obvious piece of equipment is missing. You do think that, don't you?' she went on when she realised that Pearl was not going to answer.

Pearl nodded. 'I suppose so,' she said in a subdued voice.

'Well, I don't agree. What we're looking at here is part of the great blossoming of life as a woman in the West in the last twenty years. We can deal honestly with each other in a way that isn't possible when you have a man in the picture. Who was the last man you went with?'

'I'm sorry. I can't tell you that.'

'And no more you should. How much faith would I have in your discretion about me if you told me the name of another client? But it was a man, we already know that because I'm your first woman, and you had expectations of him that he had no choice but to meet. It hasn't always been that way. Even when I was a young woman, men still saw women as objects – they could put their hands on us, touch us up and if we objected we were simply being awkward. In my mother's time – and your mother's – they could go further than that and, as long as they didn't use violence that left the woman physically marked, it was a rare jury that would convicted them of rape. I don't suppose there was one woman in twenty who hadn't had a man's hand up her skirt at the very least. The reaction to that state of affairs has been so strong and so successful that now men have to be very careful. They almost need a signed consent before putting a hand on your knee, let alone trying to get their great ugly cock into you. Those men you've been fixed up with know the score and even if they don't much care about you as a person – and, believe me, for the most part, they don't – they still have to bring into play all the trappings of a loving seduction.

'But I'm a woman and I don't have to play by those rules. I wanted someone – a date, if that's how you want to look at it – who'd look good when we were in the company of others and be a damn good shag when we weren't.'

'You wanted a sex object.'

'Yes. I did. Not just any sex object but one with a beautiful body. That's what I paid for and that's what I got. You have a problem with that?'

Pearl thought about the question. Then she started to laugh, for it was true. The honesty she was getting from Madeleine was unlike anything she'd experienced with her male clients. 'No,' she said. 'I needed you to explain it to me but now that you have I don't have a problem at all.'

Madeleine kissed her on the lips. Then she went to her bag and retrieved the second set of dildos. 'Can you think of a single reason why two women alone in a luxurious bedroom shouldn't have the pleasure of two big hard cocks? Especially when they come without the price of two men attached to them, will never go soft before the women are ready and will stop as soon as the women have had their fill?'

'No, Maddy. I can't think of a single one.'

Madeleine placed a hand between Pearl's legs and slipped a finger into her. 'Well, you certainly don't need any more lubrication.' She inserted one imitation penis into herself, strapped the harness around her, pressed Pearl's knees apart, knelt between the young woman's thighs and guided the other into her. Pearl wrapped her arms tightly around Madeleine's back and, as the two began a humping as vigorous as any Pearl had known, their lips and tongues came together. Pearl would have said beforehand that she did not relish such a furiously wet kissing. She knew now that she would have been wrong.

When it was over and Madeleine had removed the instrument of their pleasuring, they lay side by side. Madeleine's fingers rested on Pearl's mound while Pearl's hand lay on top of them. Their rapid, almost frenzied, breathing gradually calmed. Madeleine said, 'I think what you most objected to was the way I took your ass.'

'I've never let a man do that to me. I don't think I ever shall.'

'Quite right. Not unless you find one whose dick is as thin as his finger, at any rate. You still object to it from me?'

The short pause that followed mirrored yet another occasion for reflection on Pearl's part and was followed by another laugh. 'No. I really don't think I do.'

'Good. Because I'd like to have you that way again before we leave here. Have you ever been rimmed?'

'Rimmed?'

'You haven't. It's time you were. Go into the bathroom, honey, and wash that sweet tush as clean as you can.'

'Tush?'

'What is it with you English girls? Don't you understand the simplest words? Your ass, girl. Though I suppose for you that should be arse. Make it as sweet-smelling and sweet-tasting as you can. Because taste it is exactly what I intend to do.'

'Taste it!' Pearl leapt from the bed and hurried into the

bathroom. 'Oh my God!'

'You'll like it. I promise.'

And she was right. It was, surely, not possible to enjoy such a thing. And yet it was wonderful. After Madeleine's hands had pressed Pearl's bottom cheeks apart, her tongue – hot and wet – began its circular exploration, beginning on the high edges and moving with every revolution closer to the centre. Pearl's hips were gyrating long before the tongue reached its target and the closer it got, the more vigorous the gyration until it reached the very centre and then…was this possible? Could a bottom actually open simply because a tongue pressed into it? Of course it could not. And yet, it did. Not to any huge amount – you could not have got Little Boy into there without further pressure – but open it did.

And then…Pearl had just begun to regret that Madeleine had not once more placed the pillow between her thighs when she felt something even better happen for, while the tongue probed behind, a thumb entered her before and began to coax her clitoris into action – though, to tell the truth, very little coaxing was required. Pearl's orgasm was cataclysmic.

They collapsed into a tangle of limbs. 'Are you converted?' asked Madeleine.

Pearl giggled.

'The ancient Greeks used to say, "Women for babies, boys for pleasure." That was ancient Greek men, of course. I've never seen any reason why we should not reverse the formula. I suppose you're going home for Christmas?'

'Ah. Well.' And then Pearl unburdened herself of the sadness that filled her. As she described her seduction by Uncle Martin, the actions of the elders and her mother's response, she found herself once more becoming angry at the way she had been treated.

Madeleine listened in silence. Then she said, 'The bastards. How can people behave like that? It's like the Middle Ages.'

'It's how I was brought up.'

'You poor darling. So…you're not going home for Christmas.

How would you like to spend it with me and some friends?'

'What did you have in mind?'

'There's a villa on a little island in the Caribbean. Very exclusive. I wasn't going to go because I didn't want to be the only woman there without a partner. But the invitation's still open…we'd make it a private arrangement…I mean I'd pay you of course but there's no need to involve the agency. And I'd be responsible for your airfare and all the other bills.'

'I'd be grateful if you bought my ticket but there's no need to pay me anything.'

'It's a deal. We fly on the twentieth of December and stay for ten days. If you're not a lezzie when we arrive, you will be by the time we fly home.'

'There was a woman teacher at college. I knew she wanted me but I didn't think I was interested.'

'We live and learn. And now, darling, my cunt needs your attention.'

That attention took so long and absorbed both of them so totally that showering and dressing for dinner was rushed. Before they left the room, Madeleine examined Pearl. 'You look sensational, honey. An absolute dream. You'll knock them dead. Just don't forget, it's me you're with.'

Pearl had the happiest of evenings. When they were all together at the dinner table, she knew she was the centre of attention and she revelled in it. The women asked about her studies but it was difficult not to know that they were really thinking about other things – about the body beneath the clothes, and what she allowed Madeleine the privilege of doing with it. The experience of being among women only was different from how it felt to be with men – there was a sense she had never had before that she mattered as a person and not simply as an object. Was this what she wanted in future? She wasn't ready to answer that question. Giving up men and what she did with them (and what they did with her) was not something she was ready for but she now knew that loving a woman was not without possibilities. But underneath these considerations were two things that stubbornly refused to go away. One was the idea that somewhere there was a young man whose position on the male/female continuum was closer than most to the feminine end, just as hers had a lot of the masculine in it. A submissive young man in panties. Was he an impossible dream? And the other was Angus, but every time the thought of Angus surfaced in her mind she banished it. She had been drawn to Angus in a way that she had been attracted to no other man and was not now attracted to Madeleine. Angus brought with him the possibility of real, deep love. But that was foolishness. Angus and Pearl was a pairing that could never be.

Chapter 8

Lectures and tutorials were almost done for the term and Pearl's fellow-students were preparing for the holiday. Many had already left. Those who were still there made a group more tightly-knit than usual and, two days before she was due to join Madeleine at the airport, Pearl was invited to a party by Claire and Becky, two post-grad students.

The evening was well advanced and the usual drunkenness in evidence although it did not extend to Pearl or to her hosts. Claire put a hand on Pearl's arm. 'Come out into the garden.'

When they got there, Pearl shivered. 'It's cold!'

'It is,' said Claire. 'It's also private. Probably because it's cold. But this won't take long. Next term, if you want to, you'll be permitted to move out of the accommodation block and into a place of your own.'

'I know. I've had invitations.'

'You haven't accepted any?'

Pearl shook her head.

'There'll be a place here. Becky is going to the States for two years. She has a research scholarship at Yale. We'd like to offer it to you.'

'We? I thought only you and Becky lived here.'

'There's also James.'

'James? Do I know him? Is he here tonight?'

'No you don't and yes he is. He's the one in the red shirt and the waistcoat.'

'Oh,' said Pearl. 'I didn't realise he lived here. I smiled at him but he seemed awfully standoffish.'

'He can appear that way. Really, he's shy and he's shy for a reason. That reason is why Becky and I let him move in with us.'

'Now you've got my interest. You'll have to tell me.'

'James can seem a bit fey. It's misleading.' She looked at the ground, giving Pearl the impression that she was thinking, looking for the best way to say what she had to say. When her head came up, there was a determined look on her face. 'He had a lot of trouble at school.'

'Oh?'

'Not academically – he's very bright. But you know people in their teens, boys or girls it doesn't matter which, can be very censorious about people who don't fit into a mould. And James always ploughed his own furrow.'

Pearl knew there was more to the story. 'What aren't you telling me?'

'I don't know everything. James and I come from the same city but we weren't at the same school and, anyway, he's four years younger than I am. But you hear things. People said he was gay but he isn't, not that there would be anything wrong with it if he were but the simple fact is that it's women he likes and not men. Look, I feel bad talking about him this way. If you want to join us, join us. You can draw your own conclusions about James and if he likes you he'll probably tell you his story sometime anyway.'

This was a nice house and Pearl was drawn by the idea of living in it but she could see a problem. Her regular disappearances two or three weekends each month would be much more noticeable in a household of three people. She didn't want to risk discovery, however pleasant the idea of independent living might seem. And then that problem went away.

'There's something I haven't told you,' said Claire, 'and you really do need to know. I didn't seek you out by chance. Evelyn suggested I offer you a room here.' Her eyes were looking directly into Pearl's and there was the hint of a smile there.

'Ah. And you…?'

'I was recruited just as you were, though rather longer ago.'

'And Becky?'

'Her too. But not James, if you're wondering about that. He's here because Becky and I felt we could give him an easier life than most house-sharers would. So. You don't have to make up your mind right now but I would like to know as soon as possible.'

'Oh, I have no difficulty saying yes. I'm going away for Christmas; I'd like to leave some of my stuff here before I go and move in the week before term starts again.'

Claire put her arms round Pearl and hugged her. She shivered. 'Let's go in. It's freezing out here. And I think James should meet his new house mate.'

Two days later, Pearl flew in Business Class with Madeleine. She was weeks away from a spiritual and mental collapse that would leave her catatonic and others fearful for her sanity, but she did not know that then. Later she would sit in the dark, tears rolling down her cheeks as she searched for the cause of her downfall and she would wonder what part sharing had played in the catastrophe. For Madeleine had shared her with others.

But at the time she accepted it as simply part of the Christmas fun.

Or so it seemed.

Then she flew back to the excitement of a new home and new house mates.

Pearl was not a suspicious person, but she was methodical and she soon knew that something was happening to her underwear. Items – predominantly knickers – were going missing for a short while before reappearing. Sometimes they went from the laundry basket and sometimes the mislaid garment had been taken unworn from a drawer.

She decided something must be done.

James was reading in an easy chair in his bedroom when Pearl opened the door without knocking. The expression on his face when he looked up said that he was going to remonstrate with the intruder – an intention that disappeared when she held up a pair of knickers between thumb and forefinger. His face went bright red. Pearl said, 'If you're going to lose control of yourself while you've got them on, the least you can do is wash them before you put them back.'

Oh, no, she thought. He's going to cry. She stepped forward and was appalled to see James lean back in his seat as though he expected to be hit. She knelt beside him and took his hands in hers. With all the gentleness she could muster, she said,

'James. James. I'm not cross.'

'No?'

'No. Curious – yes. But cross? No.'

'I'm sorry. I knew I shouldn't, but…'

Compassion filled her heart. The poor man. What could she say? What could she do? 'James, we all have things like that. Things we shouldn't do and we know we shouldn't do them but knowing we shouldn't doesn't stop us. 'Do you want to talk about it?'

His hand swiped across his face. 'What is there to tell? You must think I'm disgusting.'

'James, if I thought that, it would show. You'd be able to tell. But I'd like to understand. Is it…do you wish you were female?'

James shook his head.

'Then what? You just like the feel?'

Another headshake. She shuffled forward a little on her knees. Quietly, as though coaxing a child or a small, shy animal she said, 'Help me out here, James.'

He sat upright but did not try to remove his hands from hers. 'It's so difficult to explain. Easy to feel, easy to be, easy to do but difficult to explain.'

'If you're willing to try, I'll listen. In case you're wondering, James, this stays between us. I haven't told Claire, haven't told anyone. And I won't.'

He nodded. 'Thank you. It's about submission. At least, I think it is.'

'Submission?'

Another nod. 'I'm not a virgin, Pearl. I've been to bed with women. Not men; I know some people think I'm gay but I've never been drawn by that.'

'No. So. Women. In bed. And?'

'Sex between men and women follows a pattern. It probably always has, since we sheltered in caves and fought lions with our bare hands. The man takes the lead. The woman submits.'

'I see. And that isn't how you want it to be?'

He shook his head.

'You want to be in a relationship, you want it to be with a woman, but you want it to be the woman who takes the lead and you who submits.'

James nodded. Pearl bent forward and kissed him. 'Well, James. I think I may have the solution for you.'

She may have been the solution to James's problem, but that didn't mean that things were easy. They had to tell Claire that they'd become an item, and then they had to work hard to ensure that she did not feel excluded. James had to get used to the idea that Pearl had another life and that she went away, often for a whole weekend, leaving him behind. Now at last he understood why Claire and Becky had so often disappeared but understanding didn't cure his loneliness.

But the good bits outweighed the bad, at least for the present. Pearl's knicker drawer was Aladdin's Cave to James. He went to bed in her nighties and under his clothes as he walked around he wore every variety of female underwear imaginable. And when they made love – which they did most nights when Pearl was home – it was always Pearl who led the way, always Pearl on top.

Chapter 9

It was March, nine weeks into a term that was going well, academically and in other ways, when Madeleine made contact. They hadn't seen each other, haven't even spoken since they hugged, kissed and parted at Heathrow on their return from the Caribbean on the second of January and now Madeleine wanted to know whether Pearl had any plans for Easter.

When Pearl went to bed that night she asked James whether he'd mind sleeping in his own room.

'You mean alone?'

'Yes, James. If you don't mind.'

'Or even if I do?'

'Don't be difficult. There's some stuff going on in my head and I'd like to work it through on my own.'

James touched her arm. 'I'm sorry, darling. Of course you're entitled to some me time. You want to talk about it?'

'I would but I don't know what I'd say. The inside of my head is a mess right now.'

That was the night the dreams started.

Pearl on her back while Madeleine and two other women explored her various orifices – two of them (including Madeleine with Little Boy) using dildos.

Pearl on her knees between the legs of someone she couldn't even remember now while someone else used lips and fingers on her bottom.

Pearl emerging from a stupor like none she had ever known. What had that been? Rohypnol? It shocked her to realise that she would not be surprised to find that these successful, balanced, autonomous women would use a date rape drug to get what they wanted. And what *was* it they wanted? If some man had treated a teenage girl like that, the judge would have called it "abuse of the worst possible kind". But on that island with those people you smiled and did what people wanted you to do. She was paid for. A chattel. Wasn't she? She remembered what she had felt at Christmas: that among women she mattered as a person and not simply as an object.

The feeling was less strong now.

And then the devil came. Lying in bed, alone, James banished to his own room, March harsh outside the window, she looked over her shoulder and there he was. Just as he'd always been portrayed. Horned. Reptilian. Eyes gleaming in delight. "I've got you now." Just as the Brethren had warned.

She didn't get out of bed next morning. Not surprising, perhaps, except that she didn't know she hadn't got out of bed. Hours telescoped, days compressed, time passed and she knew nothing. James brought scrambled eggs and she thanked him but left them untouched. The next day was no different. On the third day, Claire decided they needed help.

The university prided itself on the quality of its pastoral care. The first visitor was staff, the next a doctor and the next someone Claire described as "a sort of psychotherapist" because how else could you describe someone like that? They talked to Claire and James because Pearl no longer spoke to anyone. When she was removed to hospital to be fed and hydrated intravenously, Claire told James they had to gather her clothes together and hide them. James wanted to know why.

'She's supposed to be a student. She lives on student loans and what she earns in the bar.'

'Bar? She never goes near the bar.'

'But that's what she told her father,' said Claire. 'So how to explain the kind of clothes she wears on dates? Where did the money come from to pay for those? The hospital has sent for her parents. Her mother will take one look at that stuff and know exactly what her daughter's been doing. We're not going to steal it – it will all be here when she's herself again – but all we can leave in this room is jeans and T-shirts and plain cotton undies. And no make-up. Girls in her church don't wear it.'

It was a tearful scene when Pearl's mother and father came to the house to collect her things. Claire showed them the room and asked for news. James had been banished in case these religious people took offence at the idea that their daughter shared a house with a man. 'She's shared a lot more with me than just a house,' said James.

'Yes, you and a lot of other people but they don't need to know about that.'

'The university is being very good,' said Pearl's father. 'Her course is suspended. She can take it up again soon as she's well.'

Pearl's mother snorted and said something that only her husband could hear but Claire was fairly sure she was saying that her daughter should never return. Claire said, 'Please give me your address so that I can write to her.'

And then they were gone. When James came back he said, 'The house seems empty without her.'

'Yes. She filled a space. I hope she gets better.'

Her father talked to Pearl on the drive home and went on talking even though she said not a word in reply. Her mother also spoke, but to him and not to her daughter. Her father said, 'We're going to try to keep you at home, love. But that means you're going to have to do your best to eat something. The doctor at the hospital says you can if you want to.'

Her mother said, 'That Claire girl knows what's going on.'

Her father said, 'And when you're feeling better, if you want to, you can come back and finish your course and get your degree.'

Her mother said, 'That business with Martin is at the bottom of this. This is shame. She knew she was doing wrong and it's caught up with her.'

Her father said, 'When we get home, you can decide whether you want to go to bed or stay up for a while. Granddad is in a home now, so there's plenty of room again. Maybe all you need is to sit with the people who love you. Did something happen, petal? Something too awful to think about?'

But there was no answer.

It's easy to assume, when someone stares blankly at nothing for hour after hour and doesn't say a word, that they have lost their senses. That the lights are on but no one's home. In fact, Pearl's mind was in ferment. She heard every word that was spoken to her and she understood. But what was she going to say? That the devil had taken control of her mind, granted access by her sustained and deliberate immorality? That the antics of a group of women at Christmas, on the face of it harmless fun unconstrained by outdated rules that had, in any case, been imposed by a patriarchal society had in fact been so empty of affection, compassion and love that they had caused her to wonder what was the point of carrying on living? She'd have struggled to say those things to anyone. To say them to her parents was impossible.

And so she said nothing. Saying nothing was the easiest thing. When people thought you had lost your marbles, what you actually gave up was responsibility. Pearl liked the idea of a little time without responsibility.

That would change, but the change would take time.

Chapter 10

Three years. Her father would think of them as the worst time in his life, her mother would remember them with fury but for Pearl they were simply three wasted years.

There were milestones that increased her mother's anger, for her mother believed that Pearl knew exactly what she was doing and that what she was doing was being deliberately unhelpful, but that her father would remember in the same way as he remembered childhood progress – the first smile, the first time she stood upright without support, the first few steps she walked on her own. After a few weeks, Pearl took the knife and fork in her hands instead of being fed by others with a spoon. A few weeks more and she walked to the end of the road and back. She had been at home for four months when she spoke for the first time. It pleased her father that those first words were "Thank you".

They learned not to ask what had happened or if there was anything she wanted to talk about because when they did that she clammed up and she could go for days without speaking again.

While she had been, as far as anyone could tell, catatonic her parents' conversation had been unguarded. Pearl had learned that the brethren had given her parents a dispensation so long as she was – in their terms – mentally incompetent. When that changed, the dispensation would come to an end and unless she repented they would once again be prohibited from breaking bread with her. She had learned a number of other things, too. The hospital and the university had recommended psychotherapy but that was completely unacceptable to the brethren who believed that the only therapy anyone needed was to study the word of God. And then there was this:

'You keep talking about her going back to university when she gets better and finishing her degree,' said her mother. 'It was university that made her like this in the first place. What she needs is to repent and be taken out of discipline and find a good man to marry and raise a family with.'

'That's for her to decide,' said her father.

'She hasn't shown any ability to make good decisions so far. It's time we intervened and made them for her.'

'Do you want to drive her away completely?'

'It's irrelevant in any case. Everyone knows what she did with Martin. What decent boy is going to want anything to do with her?'

'What she did with Martin? Don't you mean what Martin did with her?'

'Oh, please. It's always the woman. He was wrong to fall, but who put temptation in his way? She did.'

One day, a fairly balanced day for Pearl, while her mother was out shopping her father sat beside her and took her hand. 'When we brought you home, I asked the post office to start forwarding your mail here. They wouldn't do it without your signature and obviously I wasn't going to forge it but your friend Claire agreed to send it. I'm sorry, petal, but I opened one of your bank statements.'

A cold hand closed around Pearl's heart.

'I could lie and say I thought it was addressed to me but you'd know that wasn't true. That's an awful lot of money, Pearl.'

'Does Mummy know?'

'No. And after I'd seen what was in it I telephoned Claire and asked her to send bank statements to my office address.'

'Thank you.'

'I'm not going to ask where the money came from. But you need to know that if you ever want to talk to me, I'm here.'

When she turned to look at him, her eyes were filled with tears. 'Could you speak to the elders for me?'

'Of course, darling. What do you want me to say?'

'Tell them I'm ready to repent.'

He put his arms around her and hugged her tight. 'I don't know whether you will be doing it for the right reasons but I want you to know I'll be very glad to have my family whole again.'

The experience was embarrassing but it was done. After her formal act of repentance she was welcomed back into the congregation on Sunday and all of the brethren were asked to pray for her. Her father was pleased, her mother was pleased but Pearl knew the truth: that she had repented for no reason other than to make her father's life easier. The brethren had prayed over her and welcomed her back into the fold but she knew that to them she was irredeemably tainted. And they were right. She had sinned and the devil still held her.

When the elders suggested that she should attend the young people's gatherings on Sunday afternoons it was not really a suggestion. She obeyed. In theory, these meetings were for prayer and Bible study; in practice they were a way for young men and women to meet young women and men with whom they could safely fall in love and plan a future together within a congregation that would keep them on the straight and narrow. Pearl watched the pairing off and the development of chaste friendships that would one day lead to more. No boy ever suggested that he and Pearl might want to meet in other places at other times. What would a young man's parents say if he told them he was to date a scarlet woman?

And how would she feel being courted by one of these boys (she could not bring herself to think of them as men)? She replayed in her mind time after time the dates she *had* been on – starting with Desmond Payne and working through the whole sequence. It had been fun. Had it not? But look where it had brought her. She wished she could get the cork back into the bottle and return to the time of innocence when all that mattered was what she had learned from the brethren. But she could not. Every one of those couplings had been sinful. Wrong.

Except with Angus.

Yet even that exception was one she could not allow herself. She had felt an affection, a tenderness for Angus that could so easily have turned into love but people like Angus were not allowed people like Pearl – someone with family and expectations like his would be expected to marry a woman from their own background. And, even if that were not so (and it was), she had to face the reality: that her time with Angus had been an act of prostitution. Exactly the same as all the others. And he (and certainly his mother) knew that. She had to put Angus out of her mind.

As for James, no money had changed hands there and she had enjoyed what they had done together but was he really someone she would want to spend her life with? He was not.

As she processed these thoughts, she understood what she was doing. She was looking at how she wanted to spend the next phase of her life and it was not going to resemble the last three years.

It was July. A new university term would begin soon. She had been promised that there was a place there for her once more when she was well.

So what was wrong with her? She thought about it and she realised that she *was* well, or at least well enough to go to university – if she wanted to be. The freedom granted by that rider astonished her. She was well if she wanted to be. She could resume her life if she wanted to. Her past would still be there, the devil would retain his hold, she would still be stained blood-red by sin but if she wanted to go back to university and finish her degree there was nothing to stop her. Except perhaps, she reflected, her mother's opposition to the idea. Well, Pearl was twenty-one now, she had enough money in the bank to support herself during her studies and if she chose to defy her mother, she could.

Joy surged through her. She had lost three years of her life but she didn't have to lose the rest. She was older now and there were some rules by which she would live. If Evelyn and Sandra (or whoever had replaced Evelyn and Sandra) came knocking, she would show no interest in their proposals. She would spend the time in reading and study. She would avoid the student bars as she always had. And she would be celibate. She began to sing.

She was still singing when her brother Richard came in. Richard was on holiday at the end of his second year as an engineering student – university, in her mother's eyes, was so much less dangerous for a boy than for a girl. In any case, Richard would need a good job to support his family when he had one whereas Pearl's future should be in feeding her husband, keeping his home clean and looking after his children. To hell with that, she told herself.

'That doesn't sound like a hymn, sister dear,' said Richard. 'Better not let the elders hear you singing something so frivolous. You'll be on bread and water for a week.'

'Is that the sound of rebellion I hear?'

'Oh, you know.'

'Two years in the big bad world and you're questioning what you were brought up to believe?'

'Something like that. When you were at uni, did you have a boyfriend?'

'Don't be nosy.'

'I'll take that as a yes. Difficult, isn't it? When you're in love with someone the brethren would not approve of?'

'In love – those are big words. I'm not sure I ever reached that stage. What's her name?'

'Bridget.'

Pearl clapped her hand to her mouth. 'Oh, Richard. Oh, dear.'

'Yes. She's a Catholic.'

Pearl was still laughing when the door opened and her father walked in. His face radiated happiness at the sight of his daughter convulsed by merriment. 'Pearl! Something has made you laugh. Tell me!'

'Oh, I can't, Daddy. It isn't my secret to tell.'

His face turned to Richard. 'A secret?'

Richard took a deep breath. 'We were talking about my girlfriend, Dad.'

'Yes?'

'My Catholic girlfriend.'

The smile faded from their father's face. 'Yes. Right. I see. Look – can you leave it to me to break this to your mother? And maybe not today? I need to find a good time.'

'There'll never be a good time for that,' said Richard.

'No. No, you may be right. Nevertheless, don't go telling her yourself?'

'Okay, Dad.'

Her father turned to look at her. 'I haven't seen you this happy since I don't remember when. Did something happen?'

'I've decided to go back to uni.'

He nodded. 'Well, I'm pleased. But it's something else I'm going to have trouble over from your mother.'

'I'm sorry.'

'Don't be. I'll handle it. If it's any comfort, I think you're making the right decision.'

'There's something else, Daddy. If there's going to be a row, we might as well get it all out of the way in one go.'

Her father's expression said that he expected a hammer blow and that he was afraid he knew what it would be.

'I'm leaving the brethren. I'm not going back into a church that treats me the way they do. I realise that when I don't show up they'll put me under discipline and they'll say I can't eat with the rest of you so we'll keep this under wraps until I leave for the new term but after that…if they think I'm a heathen, that's what I'll be.'

Her father sat down heavily.

'Dad,' said Richard, 'it's time I made the same decision. I'm sorry, but a church that won't even consider a girl I know to be wonderful because she was brought up in a different faith is not the church for me.'

Their father put his head in his hands. 'Okay. Okay. But we won't talk about this in front of your mother. Promise me?'

Pearl said, 'Don't you ever have doubts?'

'Oh, Pearl. Doubts are what faith is about. You believe in something you know is true but can't be proved. Of course you have doubts from time to time. But God understands that. He made us what we are. God will not condemn me because sometimes I wonder if he really exists.'

'No,' said Richard. 'And he won't condemn me because I love someone who worships Him in a different way.'

'All I want is for you both to be happy.'

'And you?' said Pearl. 'Are you happy?'

'Oh, Pearl. Your mother and I have been married for twenty-four years. I had my moments of rebellion, just as you two are having now, but your mother is very firm in her ideas and when I married her I chose to put those questions behind me.'

Pearl put her arms round him. 'You're a wonderful dad. I love you. We both love you. And we'll be as good as you need us to be until we go back to uni. But after that you're going to have to visit me there, as you did once before, because if Mummy won't let me eat at the same table…'

'…and she won't…'

'…then I won't come here again. I'm not rejecting God. I'm rejecting the twisted way the brethren present him. And when you come to visit, there's no need to splash out on a place like Marianne's. I know a cheap Italian that does very good lasagne.'

Chapter 11

The university's pride in its pastoral care was well-founded. Pearl was asked whether she wanted to live in hall or in a private let and she decided that, this time, she would take the private house from the beginning. She had more than enough money to pay the rent and other expenses. She needed to manage the question of who she lived with – no drunks, no wild parties, no temptations to stray sexually. She knew she was still the sexual being she had always been and she wanted to make sure that, when she gave herself once more, it would be out of love.

She had written to Claire to say that she was returning and that there was no need to continue forwarding her mail. Claire wrote back immediately. James had taken his degree and left, Becky had returned from Yale and taken a teaching position at the university which left one room free. Would Pearl like it?

In a move that reminded her of the conversation with Martin when he told her that, to save his own skin, he had exposed her to the elders as a wanton seductress, she left the house to find a phone box from which she could call Claire. She'd like the room because she liked the women she would share the house with but she needed to get something straight. 'I'm not going back on the game. No midweek dates. No weekends away. No dinners at Marianne's with a bedroom assignation afterwards. Mechanical sex where all you care about is the technique is fine when you're in your teens but I'm not making love to anyone again until making love is what I'm doing. If the emotional connection isn't there, the physical connection won't be, either.'

She could hear the amusement in Claire's voice. 'Pearl. No one expects an escort to do it for ever. I only take very occasional gigs myself now – when it's someone I've been with before and liked and they ask specially for me.'

'There's no pressure to keep going? No blackmail?'

'There'd be no point. What the agency sells is a completely willing escort. Someone who enjoys the experience as much as the client. Their business would soon disappear if punters could see that the girl was there under duress.'

'Okay. I'll take the room.'

'All your clothes are still here.'

'Well, good. But I don't think I'll have much use for many of them.'

It was great to be back. Her tutor and the other lecturers took great care to treat her as a normal student and not as a breakable piece of glass. Her fellow students were almost all two years younger and they knew that her course had been interrupted but she turned questions aside. She completed her two remaining years and graduated with the only First to be awarded in History that year. She was asked if she would like to stay on as a postgraduate researcher. Pearl had developed a strong interest in relations during the 1900s between anti-government elements in British society and the nascent revolutionary movement in Russia and she accepted the offer gratefully.

And that was when her past returned to throw her life into turmoil.

Claire and Becky were throwing a party and Pearl agreed to be there. There would be no undergraduates; everyone invited was on the teaching staff or in postgraduate research. The party had been going for more than two hours and Pearl was enjoying herself chatting to people from all over the world who shared her lust for knowledge when the door opened and she found herself looking across the room at Angus.

And Angus found himself looking at Pearl.

It must have been obvious to everyone in the room that something was going on because it was as though a passage opened through the party throng but Pearl was oblivious to the thoughts of others. One moment Angus was in the doorway and Pearl was on the opposite side of the room. The next, they had met in the centre and were holding hands and staring into each other's eyes. The buzz of a successful party, which had been at high levels a moment ago, was now almost stilled. The two stayed like that, unconscious of anyone else's attention, until Claire put her arm around Pearl's shoulder. 'Take him into the garden, sweetheart. I don't know who he is but it's clear that you do. I'll keep everyone else away.' Pearl and Angus walked hand-in-hand across the room, through the kitchen and out of the back door into the garden in which the house windows gave enough light to see each other but not much more.

They both spoke at once. 'What are you doing here?' asked Pearl at the same time as Angus said, 'I can't believe it.' Then Angus said, 'I'm sorry. You first,' and Pearl repeated, 'What are you doing here?'

'After I got my degree,' said Angus, 'Pa said now I should go to Cirencester and learn how to run the family estates, which is what he'd wanted me to do in the first place, but I said we had plenty of managers who were ex-Cirencester and I'd find it more interesting to pursue my studies with a Masters. So I did that. Then Pa raised the question of Cirencester again but I said I wanted to go on to a Doctorate. Pa grumbled a bit but Mother talked him round. This is the best place for advanced research in my field, so here I am for at least five years. And you?'

'My studies were interrupted for a while,' said Pearl. 'I don't particularly want to talk about that. I came back, finished the course and now I'm doing my Masters.'

'Then we'll see a lot of each other,' said Angus. He looked serious. 'I tried to find you. You weren't here. I told Mother and she got a private eye on the job and I think she found something but Mother refused to tell me what it was.'

'Why did you want to find me?'

'Well, if you don't mind me saying so that's a silly question for someone bright enough to be doing postgrad research at this place. I wanted to find you because I knew you were the one for me. And the more girls I came to know, the more certain I was.'

'You didn't tell your mother that, surely?'

'Of course I did.'

Pearl found herself struggling to understand. Surely, if Lady X had thought her Viscount son had fallen seriously for a harlot, she would have done all in her power to prevent it? But perhaps she had decided to let the two come together again so that Angus could get over his infatuation and realise that Pearl would not do. But if she'd wanted that, and if her private detective had told her what she presumably had told her, surely Lady X would have passed that information to Angus as a certain passion killer? It was impossible to understand.

'It's cold out here,' said Pearl. 'Shall we rejoin the others?'

'I'd rather be only with you. I just found you after all this time and I don't want to share you.'

'We'd better go to my room, then,' said Pearl.

She was aware of the chatter as they passed once more through the room and then started up the stairs. When they reached her room, Pearl felt awkward. She did not want to go near the bed, so she sat on her dressing table stool and signalled for Angus to take the only chair. She said, 'There's something you need to know. I don't do what I used to do. I haven't been to bed with a man for five years.' She held his eye. 'Or a woman.'

Angus looked once more like the young boy he had seemed to be when they had first met and she had asked if he'd like to undress her. 'I'm so glad. I'd hate to think of you with other men.'

It was time for honesty. 'That's what I did, Angus. That's how we came to meet. Your parents paid me.' She took a deep breath because she hated what she was going to say but it needed to be said. 'I was a prostitute.'

'And now you're not,' said Angus, as though what she had just said was of no importance to him at all. 'Will you have dinner with me tomorrow? I believe Marianne's is very good but I haven't had a chance to try it yet.'

'Angus, were you listening to me? The woman you're asking to dinner used to be a whore.'

'And she hasn't been to bed with a man for five years. Or a woman,' he added with a wry smile and Pearl said, 'Oh, you were listening, then,' and Angus said, 'Were you? I said I've looked for you all these years because I knew you were the person for me. Is it likely I'll be put off by the idea of what you did five years ago? Marianne's? Tomorrow?'

Well, it couldn't do any harm and when he realised that she was not, after all, the right woman for him she would at least have had a decent meal. 'Marianne's. Tomorrow. And now I find I'm suddenly very tired. Do you mind if I ask you to go? Only I need to get into bed and sleep. Alone,' she added.

'I'll pick you up at eight tomorrow evening.' He stood. 'Have you stopped kissing men as well? Because a chaste peck on the cheek would be welcome.'

She smiled, got up off the stool, took his arms in her hands and kissed him lightly, first on the cheek and then on the lips. She stepped away from him. 'Thank you for being so understanding.'

Not long after that, Pearl was in bed. She had spoken the truth when she said she was tired but still it was some time before she drifted into sleep. Her mind and her heart were both churning, though for different reasons. In her mind she was amazed by the change in Angus who, since they had last met, had become a confident adult. Her heart, though, was disturbed by something else. When she had thought of Angus during what she now termed her missing years, it had been with the fond recollection of someone with whom, had their lives been different, she could have fallen in love and grown old. What made her tremble now was the feeling – in fact, the certainty – that she *was* in love with him.

She knew this could not be. It was not fair on him and, in any case, his parents would not allow it. There was no future in their relationship. Just before she finally fell asleep she came up with a conclusion to that: if it had no future, then why not let the relationship happen? Enjoy it while it was there and mourn it when it was gone?

So often, when Pearl examined what she was feeling, she would use words like, "Underneath it all" or "Behind everything" to describe what was happening in her heart behind what was happening in her heart. This time, what was happening "under everything else" felt very much like the return of lust. She wanted to be in bed with Angus. She wanted them to be naked. She wanted to be making love with him.

And she did not want to be the one on top.

It was later than usual next morning when Pearl went downstairs for breakfast and Claire and Becky had already eaten but they had not left the kitchen. They wanted news. 'Who was he?' 'You obviously knew each other – from where?' 'Are you seeing him again?' 'He's gorgeous. Has he got a brother?'

It came to Pearl that Angus was, in fact, gorgeous or at least – since she did not think much of that as a way to describe someone who had become a very masculine man – he was very good-looking and she wondered that she had never noticed that before. Had he seemed too much of a boy when she had known him earlier? He certainly could not be described that way now.

She answered their questions, to the extent that she wanted to, while she scrambled eggs and fried bacon. 'I've got a kidney in the fridge if you'd like it,' said Becky and Pearl, accepting the offer, remembered how hungry she had been the morning after Desmond Payne had initiated her into the work of a call girl. Claire put a pot of Dijon mustard beside her plate. 'You can't eat that without mustard. It wouldn't be civilised. Now. When are you seeing him again'

'Tonight. He's picking me up at eight.'

'Going somewhere nice?'

'Marianne's.'

'My word! That's a pricey place for a doctoral student. Are you paying?'

Putting down her toast, Pearl shook her head. 'He's a Viscount. One day, he'll be a Duke.'

'Oh my God,' said Becky. 'And he loves you to bits, doesn't he? It's written all over him.'

'He says he does,' said Pearl.

'And you love him,' said Claire.

'Yes. I rather think I do. But his parents won't allow a match between us, so I'm just going to go with the flow and enjoy it while I can and rely on friends like you to pick up the pieces afterwards.'

It was, she supposed, a courtship. They saw each other every day, even if sometimes it was only in college – hers or his – for a coffee because one or both of them was under too much time pressure academically to allow more. However much in love they were, both of them wanted the best academic results possible. At least three days a week, they walked – by the river, across nearby fields or, taking advantage of Angus's Aston Martin (which when she first saw it brought into Pearl's mind the recollection – at the time so enjoyable and now unpleasant even to think about – of her first weekend with Madeleine) to towns and countryside further afield. They took picnics and ate in country pubs. They held hands. Whenever they were together, Pearl was conscious of the desire for consummation – the yearning to lie naked in Angus's arms and give herself to him. It was five weeks before she could stand it no longer and afterwards she would congratulate herself on the strength of will that had let her hold out for so long.

They had returned from a drive to the Malvern Hills. Becky and Claire were at some party or other. They had eaten lunch that day in a pub whose chef had previously worked at a restaurant with two Michelin stars and for supper Pearl had laid on the table a spread of salami, chorizo, lettuce, tomatoes, hard-boiled eggs, olives and the mayonnaise she made herself. When they had eaten all they wanted, Pearl put the remainder in the fridge and the dishes in the dishwasher. She turned to look at Angus. Her mind churned with uncertainty. Angus had never given the slightest indication that he wanted her as she wanted him. How would he take this? Would it be the end of their relationship? Well, she had to know. 'Do you remember when I asked if you'd like to undress me?'

'I do.' It was said in a whisper, the first sign of shyness since they had met again.

'Would you like to do it again?'

He stood up, folded her into his arms and kissed her. 'I'd like that more than anything.' Once again, the voice was subdued.

They went upstairs hand-in-hand. Angus closed the door behind them as she raised her arms to enfold him. They kissed. Angus picked her up and laid her on the bed. She said, 'I'm on the pill, darling. I started taking it again the morning after you came to the party. You don't have to worry. I'm not trying to trap you by getting pregnant.'

He sat back on his heels, looking at her. 'Is that what you think I think?'

'Well, I worry…'

'Honestly, Pearl. I sometimes think you're having a relation-ship with me that I'm not in.' He started on the buttons of her blouse.

It was some time later that calm returned to Pearl's bedroom. The two of them lay naked and closely entwined. Pearl was conscious of feeling utterly at peace for the first time in years. Then she amended that: she was at peace for the first time in her life.

Angus said, 'That was wonderful. Thank you.'

'It was, wasn't it? You must've had a damn good teacher.'

'The very best. So good, I fell in love with her and it's never gone away.'

It wanted two weeks to Christmas when Angus asked Pearl to spend it at his home. She said, 'I can't do that, darling.'

'I'm sorry. Of course you'll want to be at home yourself. Is that a chance for me to meet your parents?'

For the first time since her father had told her that he had opened her bank statement, the cold hand closed around Pearl's heart. 'Why would you want to do that?'

Clearly, Angus was bewildered. 'So that I can ask your father for your hand, of course. Don't you feel the same way?'

Pearl was shaking. This was impossible. 'Darling. My parents would hate you because you're not one of the breth-ren. And you wouldn't like them. And in any case, I'm not going home for Christmas because I'm no longer one of the brethren either, which means they are not allowed to sit at the same table with me for meals.'

'You can't be serious. Why have you never said anything about this?'

'Probably because it hurts too much. Because I don't like telling people who matter to me just how small-minded and petty my mother is.'

'Just your mother? What about your father?'

'Oh, he'd like it all to go away, but he can't fight my mother. Not on religion. That's her ground, not his.'

'Well, I never heard any of this. Do you think you should tell me the whole story?'

And so she did, and it was some time before Angus was able to make his pitch again. 'So,' he said. 'If you're not going home for Christmas, and you're not going anywhere else, why can't you come to us?'

How was she going to answer this? With the truth, she supposed. Nothing else was going to do. 'Darling,' she said. 'You are who you are. What you are, I suppose I should say. And your parents are who they are. And I'm a girl of no account from a potty little dissenting family in a town that most of the population couldn't find on a map. What we have is wonderful, but your parents are never going to allow it to be permanent. They are never going to let us marry.'

Angus was staring at her. 'Oh. I see. Well, if my parents won't want you as a daughter-in-law we'd better forget about Christmas.' He left not long after that and Pearl did not see him or hear from him the next day. She assumed that he had allowed her to introduce him to the real world and that she had better start getting used to being on her own again. The thought made her very sad.

The day after that, a letter arrived just in time for Pearl to read it before she left home for a meeting with her supervisor.

When she came out of the meeting, Angus was sitting on the wall, waiting. 'Well?'

'I had a letter from your mother.'

'I know that. That's why I said "Well?" So. Well?'

'I thought my family were the mad ones. Clearly, I had no idea.'

'Pearl. May I tell my mother that we will be one more for the holiday?'

'Yes, Angus. You may.'

'And shall I tell her that you will need a bedroom of your own?'

'No, Angus. You shall not.'

'I feel like celebrating. I've never done lunch at Marianne's but I expect it's pretty good?'

'Well, why don't we put it to the test?'

Chapter 12

Her welcome when they arrived the day before Christmas Eve was even warmer than on her first visit. She had no difficulty in engineering a private conversation with Lady X for that was exactly what her ladyship wanted and Pearl went straight to the single point that most exercised her. 'Lady X.'

'Please, my dear. Alice.'

'Alice. Angus thinks he wants to marry me.'

'Yes, Pearl. My husband and I are delighted. We so hope you will accept. You would be perfect for him.'

'Alice. I was a prostitute.'

'Yes?'

'How can you possibly want a member of the aristocracy to marry a prostitute?'

Lady X began to laugh. Pearl thought it was the nicest, kindest laugh she had ever heard. 'Oh,' said Lady X, 'is that the problem? My dear. You are an historian. You must have some knowledge of how the nobility in this country have proceeded over the centuries. When was the fact that a woman had charged for her services ever a bar to entry into the aristocracy? Good heavens. Even in our own family, the branches would be denuded if we removed all the whores who had married one of our noble males. Just imagine the changes the College of Heralds would have to make – to say nothing of Debrett's – if they had to remove from the genealogical charts every woman who had ever sold her body. I'm more concerned about the break in your time at university. Would you mind telling me what that was about?'

In a voice that was halting at first but gained in force as she entered into her story, Pearl recounted the difficulties that she had lived through. It took some time and at one point Lady X waved away Angus who clearly wanted to join in the conversation. When it was over, Lady X said, 'If I understand you correctly, you considered yourself such a sinner that you were convinced the devil had taken possession of you. Is that right?'

'Essentially, yes,' said Pearl.

'Very well. What I want you to do now, please, is to think through every single one of your assignations and tell me what you did wrong.'

'What I did wrong? I slept with men I was not married to. I slept with men who were married to someone else. I lived an immoral life.'

'I hear that, my dear. But what I asked was what you thought you had done wrong?'

'But…'

'I want you to let me tell you what I think. If you don't agree, you don't agree. But I'd like you to hear it. Is that all right?'

'Yes. Of course.'

'Very well. You have been brought up to believe in a vengeful God. A God who makes rules that are almost impossible to keep and punishes those who fail. Forgive me, my dear, but that is a very difficult life to follow. In this family, we have been part of the Church of England since the Reformation. I can guess what your brethren think of the Church of England…'

'…we are taught that it is every bit as bad as the Catholic Church…'

'…but I will tell you how it feels from the inside. It feels like the personification of tolerance. Where your coreligionists exclude, the Anglicans include. Where they damn, the Anglicans pardon. Who and what they ban, the Anglicans welcome. In your childhood, it seems to me, you were given an almost endless list of rules that you must keep. Keeping them is – to say the least – difficult. You were given a licence to fail. If I were to ask your elders to justify themselves, they would give the usual dissenting answer – that they stick to what is in the Bible and only what is in the Bible.'

Pearl nodded. 'That is what they say.'

'And it is simply not true. If you were to join the Church of England, you would find that you had only two rules to keep. And those rules are, indeed, clearly stated in the Bible by no less an authority than Jesus himself. Thou shalt love the Lord thy God with all thy heart and with all thy soul. And thou shalt love thy neighbour as thyself. Those are the rules, and the only rules. Now, bearing in mind only those two rules, let me ask you again: what did you do that was wrong?'

Pearl was silent. Not because she had nothing to say but because she was thinking. She had always loved God, even after she rejected the twisted version of Him that she was given. But had she loved her neighbour as herself? Had she done that when she was sleeping with all those men? She turned the question on its head: when she had slept with all those men, at what point had she not loved her neighbour as herself? She smiled.

Lady X saw the smile. 'Have you found it possible to forgive yourself?'

'I believe you have given it to me, Alice.'

'I thank Heaven for that. And I hope that one day soon we will be able to issue invitations to the wedding of our son and a young woman who I fervently hope to see become a member of this family. Why don't you seek him out and see if he is in the mood to propose?'

And that is what she did.

Her mother refused to attend the wedding but her father and Richard came and her father gave her away. Did she and Angus live happily ever after? This is not a fairy tale. But on balance, Pearl's life was happier and more fulfilled than was normal among the brethren.

And she had many years of satisfying sex and bore Angus three beautiful children.

And she never heard from or saw the devil again.

Author's Note

First let me say that I am always delighted to hear from readers and you can contact me at kc@mandrillpress.com. Comments on the books, positive or negative, are welcome. Please feel free to enter into a dialogue with me. I also have a blog at http://www.kccarlton.com, If you've read anything else by me, or visited my blog or Goodreads page, then you already know that a book by K C Carlton (me) is sometimes a joint production by me and my brother, Jimmy.

Jimmy also wrote a number of stories that he gathered together under the title, *Taken By Force*. Jimmy had a particular and individual approach to sex. He and I were brought up with a very traditional view of the way men and women were supposed to live their lives. I followed our parents' teaching for most of my life but Jimmy was accidentally exposed at a young age to something very different and he found he liked it (he tells the whole story in *Winging It*). If I've understood what Jimmy believed, it was that everyone should feel free to do whatever they wanted as long as it did not hurt anyone else. On the face of it it's hard to argue with that, but life is rarely as simple as we would like it to be.

In any case you either enjoyed these stories or you didn't. If you did, there are some other books you might like.

Winging It by K C Carlton

Another movie star's memoir saying how wonderful everyone has been? Not quite. Jimmy Carlton leaves a successful career with the BBC for an actor's life in Hollywood where he becomes a household name and a rich man. But Jimmy has a past his fans know nothing about and Winging It shows us his life with total honesty. He is frank about the

*men and women he meets in Hollywood: the (male) produc-
er who trades a movie contract for a night with Jimmy;
the virginal goddess film star who insiders know to be a
nymphomaniac; the all-action male who always gets the
girl in the last reel but with whom Jimmy has a passionate
gay relationship. Then Jimmy comes as near to death as it's
possible to do without ending up in a mortuary. If that really
was the face of God he saw as life seemed to be ebbing
away then everything has to change. But was it?*

When you read *Winging It* it's probably as well to remember that Jimmy was bisexual. The descriptions of sex are
as graphic as you will find anywhere and that includes the
things he did with other men as well as what he did with
women. If explicit male/male sex does not appeal to you,
don't read this book.

A Perfect Solution by K C Carlton

*A Perfect Solution is the story of a young man who does not
at the beginning know whether he is gay or straight—so he
experiments until he finds his true love. There is sex in it—
but this is above all else a romance to touch the heart. Chris
is a young man brought up with three girls and a girl is what
he wishes he had been. The girls dress him as one of them
and he revels in the life that opens up for him. If you don't
want to know what it is that men do when they're in bed with
other men, you should not read this book—but Chris finds
that girls, too, are not without their attractions. He falls
in love with one, but she is denied to him; he falls in love
with another and loses her, too. In sadness he turns back to
men—but Cupid has one last card to play before Chris finds
his perfect solution.*

And, finally, another Mandrill Press book that Jimmy and I did not write but that I wish we had.

The Transformation of David *by S F Hopkins*

The Chakin teach Andrew Matthews how to transfer people between bodies. Breaking a solemn promise, he turns his daughter, Lottie into David Walters in order to seize David's fortune--and, along the way, enjoy the carnal pleasures of the beautiful female body that was forbidden him. The Chakin cross the seas to release David from his bondage as a woman, and David is grateful to them...but the gratitude is not total. Has David, in becoming a man once more, lost more than he gains?

www.ingramcontent.com/pod-product-compliance
Lightning Source LLC
Chambersburg PA
CBHW070502170726
48291CB00008B/2621